DIARY
OF A HAUNTING

DIARY OF A HAUNTING

M. VERANO

SIMON PULSE

NEW YORK   LONDON   TORONTO   SYDNEY   NEW DELHI

SIMON PULSE

An imprint of Simon & Schuster Children's Publishing Division

1230 Avenue of the Americas, New York, New York 10020

First Simon Pulse paperback edition August 2016

Text copyright © 2015 by Simon & Schuster, Inc.

Cover photographs copyright © 2015 by Monica Quintana/Arcangel Images

Photo on page 11 copyright © Getty/Stuart Fox; photo on page 22 copyright © Trevillion/Stephen Wilson; photo on page 27 copyright © iStock/Auris; photo on page 37 copyright © Trevillion/Andrew Sanderson; photos on pages 77 and 280 copyright © Shutterstock; photo on page 80 copyright © Arcangel/Hayden Very; photos on pages 119, 138, 179, 213, 227, 231, 233, 292, and 311 copyright © Thinkstock; photos on page 124 copyright © Masterfile (flies); Arcangel/Mark Owen (hands with jar); photo on page 131 copyright © Getty/Escobar Studios; photo on page 135 copyright © Getty/Stephen Webster; photo on page 152 copyright © Arcangel/Douglas Black; photo on page 257 copyright © Trevillion/Frank Losay; photo on page 263 copyright © Getty/Adam Papadatos; photo on page 271 copyright © Trevillion/Susan Fox; photo on page 275 copyright © Trevillion/Christophe Dessaigne

For information about special discounts for bulk purchases, please contact Simon & Schuster Special Sales at 1-866-506-1949 or business@simonandschuster.com.

The Simon & Schuster Speakers Bureau can bring authors to your live event. For more information or to book an event contact the Simon & Schuster Speakers Bureau at 1-866-248-3049 or visit our website at www.simonspeakers.com.

Designed by Regina Flath

The text of this book was set in Berling LT Std.

Manufactured in the United States of America

2 4 6 8 10 9 7 5 3 1

The Library of Congress has cataloged the hardcover edition as follows:

Verano, M.

Diary of a haunting / M. Verano.

pages cm

Summary: After her parents' high-profile divorce, sixteen-year-old Paige is forced to leave Los Angeles for a rambling Victorian mansion in small-town Idaho where she soon notices strange occurrences that seem to be building toward some unspeakable horror.

[1. Horror stories. 2. Haunted houses—Fiction. 3. Supernatural—Fiction. 4. Diaries—Fiction. 5. Mystery and detective stories.] I. Title.

PZ7.1.V45Di 2015

[Fic]—dc23

2015010648

ISBN 978-1-4814-3069-2 (hc)

ISBN 978-1-4814-3068-5 (pbk)

ISBN 978-1-4814-3070-8 (eBook)

EDITOR'S NOTE

For as long as I can remember, I have been fascinated by the supernatural, and for years sought any evidence of its existence. Indeed, it is for this reason that I entered academia, and began my inquiry into the peculiar faith and practice known as Pronoica. From the first I learned of it, I had a sense that there was more to this strange relic of an earlier era than was obvious at first sight—that here at last, in the story of this movement, I would find the tokens that would confirm to me, if to no one else, that there was more to this life than the mere material.

Although I caught glimpses suggestive of a shadow world beyond our own, there was nothing to render it visible to human eyes. Nothing to convince me firmly, let alone anyone else. All was evanescent—enough to breed in me a hope, a curiosity, and drive toward knowledge, but nothing I could share.

In all that time, I wished for anything that would validate my theories and make them worthy of publication. I never dreamt that what I found would come at such a terrible price.

The shocking events of this story have shaken me more than I can possibly express. I have lost . . . No. What I have lost cannot be quantified. To even try would be a terrible insult to the memory of the departed.

Nevertheless, now that this documentary evidence has fallen into my life, the tragedy that brought it to my attention cannot be reason to hide it from public knowledge. It is vital, for the sake of human understanding, that this information be released to the world. I wish that the evidence were stronger. I know that many—most, perhaps—will read this account and view it as fraud, or worse yet, as entertainment. I can only hope that a few will see this document for what it truly is: a tragic testimonial concerning the dread workings of the spirit world upon our own.

Some names have been changed to protect the privacy of the bereft.

Montague Verano, Phd.
Professor, Department of History
University of Idaho

THURSDAY, JANUARY 1, 11:14 A.M.

New year, new journal! Or well, new attempt at old journal.

I haven't posted here in forever. I can't believe I even remember the password. All my old posts are so ridiculous. I'm not even friends with those people anymore. I used to get so worked up about this or that boy, or who was passing notes in math class. All that stuff seems far away now, ever since Real Life came along and punched me in the face.

From now on I am only posting locked entries—I don't think anyone I know is still on this site anyway, but just in case. It'll be kind of a relief to have one place where I can be completely honest . . . even if it doesn't always make me look that great.

But really, it's everyone else who look like assholes right now. I just . . . I cannot believe my dad. My *dad*! The person I loved and admired most in this world, who I looked up to . . .

It's been six months, but I still can't wrap my head around the fact that he was having an affair. That now he has a new wife, that he has no interest in even seeing me and Logan anymore. I mean, he says he does, but that seemed like it was more for the judge than for us. I can hardly blame the new girl for not wanting to deal with stepkids, what with her being all of TWENTY-TWO.

Disgusting.

And the worst thing is what a cliché it is. It's not like I completely lived in a bubble. I was semi-aware that Hollywood producers don't have the greatest record of staying married to one woman their whole lives . . . especially when that woman was a beautiful young movie star when they got married. And that's exactly what all the industry rags are saying, *obviously*. It feels like everyone outside these four walls is actually *yawning* at how lame and predictable this divorce is, my dad trading Mom in for the younger version.

I don't know, I shouldn't be shocked, but I am. Call me naive, but I really believed our family was different. We used to joke about it around the dinner table, how all that Hollywood gossip would never affect us because Mom and Dad were real people, not like the stereotypical plastic LA-types. They even named me Paige and not, like, Starfruit or Crash or some absurd celebaby name. But *haha*, turns out the joke is on me. And I'm the only one who didn't see the punch line coming a mile away.

Well, me and Mom. If anyone is handling this worse than I am . . .

And that's the thing. Part of me is really glad to see her starting to get back on her feet at last. It's definitely a step up from alternately sobbing and staring off into space, or screaming into her phone at her lawyer—though that was good in a way, because it got her a fat settlement (another good thing about my parents being "real people" is they didn't have a prenup, like the rest of Hollywood). So there's that at least.

Does that sound awful?

Mercenary. That's what the New Girl called Mom, according to TMZ (which I have stopped reading, obviously, but the kids in school insist on feeding me every gross detail).

But whatever, the whole point of this journal is for me to be able to say these ugly things and not feel bad about it. So there it is: I am glad that if Dad has to be a scumbag and ruin everybody's life, at least we get some money out of it.

And I'm glad Mom is doing better. I really am. But I wish she could find a way of getting better that's less disruptive to *my* life. Haven't I been through enough upheaval this year? Now, in addition to losing my family, I'm also about to lose all my friends, my school, my room, everything that is familiar to me, all so Mom can follow her dream out in . . . God, it makes me cringe to even say it. Idaho.

IDAHO. Is that not just . . . completely psychotic or what? Is that even a real place? I guess Cassie and Mackenzie went there last year to ski, but I don't think we're moving to the ski-resort part.

SATURDAY, JANUARY 3, 9:30 A.M.

It looks like Mom really means it about this Idaho thing. We leave in less than a week!

I totally get the desire to get away from Hollywood for a while, but couldn't she have applied to graduate school in normal places? Like NYU, or London . . . or even *Seattle* or something. But I guess when you're obsessed with the environment and ecology, "middle of nowhere" is pretty much your only option. Don't get me wrong, I do think it's cool that after all those years being a stay-at-home mom, and saving owls for charity on the side, Mom is now really going for it, studying natural resource conservation so she can make the world a better place. Sure, Dad and I like (liked!) to tease her about being such a hippie-dippie do-gooder, with all her "trust the universe" and "stewards of the earth" and "law of attraction" silliness, but I really do admire her.

Maybe more now than I did when they were together.

Mom's always been such a positive, open "spirit" as she would say, and that grated on me, because I take after my dad more, with the cynical sardonic personality . . . but it was weird and kind of terrible to see her so wretched for the past few months, because it was so not her. Like living with a stranger. And now she is finally coming out of it, which is a relief, but can I just say it one more time? IDAHO. Who does that? Who does that to her innocent children? I just can't even.

Come on, where's that positivity, Paige? *deep breath*

Okay, maybe it won't be so bad. Nature, right? It's supposed to be beautiful there. Maybe I'll get to see a moose or something. And it will make Mom happy. That's the important thing.

Thursday, January 8, 10:04 p.m.

Having serious second thoughts about this Idaho business. I cannot believe that this morning I woke up to 70-degree cloudless weather, and willingly got on a plane to take me to *this*. Though saying "willing" might be a slight overstatement.

I am trying to put a good face on everything for Mom and Logan, but holy crap, it is miserable here. For the past few days Mom has been feeding us fantasies of our first real snowfall, and how we were going to make snowmen and snow angels and have snowball fights. I admit I was getting a teensy bit excited about going to this winter wonderland. Then we get off the plane and we're greeted with *slush*. Dirty wet slush that gets in your shoes and soaks the bottoms of your jeans. And wind! I have never felt so much wind. It's like being on a mountaintop even when you're in the middle of downtown. Not that there *is* a downtown, really. Just one street with a few college bars I can't set foot in. Plus an indie movie theater, an indie bookstore—Jesus, hasn't anyone heard of chain stores here? Apparently Barnes and Noble hasn't made it to the frontier.

Our new house is a big hulking gray monstrosity, which is what you get when you rent a place sight unseen from six states away. Though you could almost imagine it being kind of pretty, once upon a time, with the big wraparound porch and the little turret on one side. If it were in better shape, it might look like something out of a storybook. Inside, everything is centered around a big staircase, and there's a massive room on the first floor that I guess was once a ballroom? Crazy. Mom and I agreed to leave that room empty because we would be, like, shouting at each other across it. There is a smaller room with a nice fireplace that I think we'll make the living room. In the back is a kitchen, which is pretty small compared to our place back in California, though it does have a big pantry behind it. Then another couple of random rooms, one of which will be Mom's study, and the others will inevitably fill up with junk, I bet.

It must have been a mansion when it was built, probably a million years ago, but now it's just old and rickety. And drafty. They don't seem to have heard of insulation here. The wind whistles through the walls so much that you can feel it indoors. Even with the heat all the way on and my heaviest sweater, it still feels like I'm standing outside. Except when I *am* outside, and it feels like I'm in Siberia. And so far the moving truck hasn't arrived with our stuff yet, so in the meantime we are making do with just sleeping bags and air mattresses. Logan thinks camping indoors is awesome. Wish I could share his enthusiasm . . .

The house is on the outskirts of town, though to be honest

that's only about a mile from the, uh, inskirts of town. On one side it's a normal street with other houses and cars and stuff, but you go around back and the town just ends. Normally don't cities and towns sort of peter out, the houses getting farther apart from one another until eventually you are looking at open fields? Not here. Step out into the backyard and you can see for miles. Not that there's anything to see.

Before I came, I spent some time looking up pictures of Idaho online, and there were all these super pretty landscapes of snowcapped mountains and crystal clear lakes. Well, that must be some other Idaho, because all we've got here are these weird little stubbly brown hills, extending out all the way to the horizon. And nothing on them—no houses, no trees, no roads, just the occasional broken-down barn, or the towering shape of a grain elevator outlined against the sky. Oh, and the sky here isn't blue. It isn't even gray. It's pure white like cotton, and it seems to go on forever. Makes the whole world feel sort of muffled.

That's what I see from my window. At first I wanted the room at the front of the house, under the turret, but Logan claimed it on his run through. Mom shot a look over at me— on the plane she had promised me first dibs on the rooms, since I'm older (and maybe since I'd been whining about the move)—but it didn't feel right pulling rank. Not when Logan seemed so excited. Plus, there was something weird about that room. I don't know what it was, but the minute I walked in, I felt this sort of buzzing, like a vibration coming up through the floor, or maybe through the air even. It set my teeth on edge, and after just a few minutes helping Logan dust the place, I had a bit of a headache. I wonder if there's some kind of transformer or something just outside? But Logan and Mom didn't seem to notice it.

Anyway, after that I was just as happy to pick a room at the back of the house, even if it's a little smaller and looks out over those endless brown hills.

FRIDAY, JANUARY 9, 9:37 A.M.

The house is infested with vermin.

I don't know why I didn't notice it the first day. Maybe they were in hiding? But today they definitely sent out the welcoming committee.

I went out early this morning for a run (bad idea, btw— all that slush from the other day had frozen overnight into a solid sheet of gray ice), and when I came back in through the front door, I felt something tugging on my ponytail. At first I thought it must be Logan messing with me, so I yelled "quit it" and turn around to swat him away, and that's when I see some *thing* caught in my hair. Ugh.

Just inside the front door, there are these three sticky, yellow-orangey strips hanging from the ceiling—right where anyone walking in would get snagged on them. Mom says

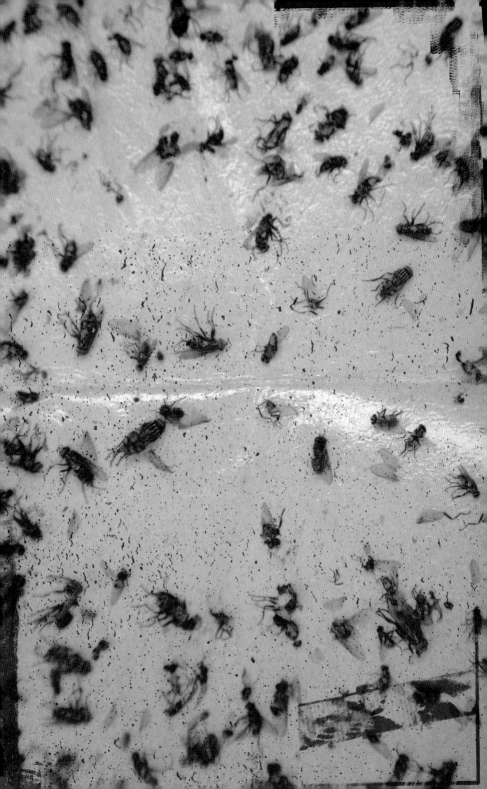

it's flypaper, which I've heard of but never seen before, and she says she hasn't seen it since she was a kid. How do we deal with flies in the civilized world? I don't know, but we must somehow, because you hardly ever saw them in California.

Anyway, I let out a yelp, which brings Mom to my rescue. She manages to disentangle me, and we both look closer and realize the strip is *covered* in flies. Dead fly bodies, all up in my hair. That's cool, I guess.

So obviously I scuttle away in revulsion while Mom says not to worry because she is going to take the strips down. And Logan, who must have been drawn like a moth to the bright light of my discomfort, shows up and is like, but then won't there be more flies? But Mom says no, it's the middle of winter, there's no need for flypaper now. That it must be left over from summer.

"So why are these ones moving?" says Logan. And I am so sure he is messing with me that I lean over to look and it's true. It's. *True.* Flies with their wings stuck to the paper, and their wretched little legs waving around in the air.

"That's weird," says Mom, ever so helpfully.

She thinks she's an expert in all things to do with nature, but apparently she skipped the chapter on the life cycle of winged insects. But of course I know what's coming next. Mom is all upset, not because there are half-dead zombie flies in our house, but because she is *concerned* for the welfare of the flies. Yes. So she goes off on a huge speech about how cruel flypaper is, and how flies are living creatures who feel pain and fear death, and okay fine, now I am feeling kind of bad, because I see her point, but still. Ew.

So she declares, no more flypaper, nor any other poison or anything that could harm the flies. Come summer, she'll have someone take a look at making the screen door fit a little tighter, and that, according to her, should solve the problem. We'll see.

SUNDAY, JANUARY 11, 11:14 A.M.

First day of school tomorrow. Mom is the happiest I have seen her in ages, getting all her stuff ready to start classes. What a lunatic! Did she not get the memo about how all normal people dread school? But maybe it's different when you get to go by choice, instead of people forcing you.

I'm still working on being cheerful and supportive about everything, but it is hard not to be homesick for my queen-size bed and big closets and sunshine and our pool. No one has a pool here, because it is the North Pole, basically.

Oh well, better make the best of it. I can only hope school tomorrow won't be too awful.

Oh, who am I kidding? Getting plopped down in the middle of junior year in a school where everyone has probably known each other since birth? It's going to be excruciating.

MONDAY, JANUARY 12, 6:40 P.M.

Okay, so it wasn't that bad. Wow! Imagine that. This journal was supposed to be a place for all my bad thoughts, but I have to be honest and admit I had an okay time at school today. Yes, it's true that everyone here has known each other since forever, but weirdly that kind of worked in my favor. "The new girl from LA" was the big news all over the whole school, and everyone wanted to meet me. And they were all super nice! So strange . . . is this how people act outside of LA? Because at my old school we pretty much shunned any new person for at least a month or two.

Anyway, I could get used to this. I got invited to sit at the cool girl table—not LA cool, but within the context of Idaho I could tell it was the best of the available options. And they wanted to know all about Hollywood and what celeb parties I had gone to. Oh, and there was this ridiculously cute guy in my math class, so I flirted with him a little, and after school he came up and asked me if I needed a ride home! Which I couldn't accept, unfortunately, because Mom was going to pick me up and take me out for coffee and a chat about my first day, but still.

I don't know. It's not home, but it's nice to be thought of as special and exciting.

WEDNESDAY, JANUARY 14, 4:10 P.M.

Well! Scratch that last post. Everyone at school hates me now.

I guess that cute guy in my math class is dating one of the girls from the cool table. I don't know how I was expected to know that, but now she hates me, and told everyone that I am stuck-up and slutty. And everyone in school believes her, because that's what it means to be the cool girl. Everyone just unthinkingly goes along with whatever you say.

So now in addition to living in the middle of nowhere, I am also a social pariah. Fun!

In other wonderful news, it was a big mistake for Mom to take down those fly strips because the front entryway has now become Grand Central Station for flies. Big black, ugly suckers too. They've taken to hanging out in a lazy swarm right inside the front door, so it's impossible to go in or out of the house without wading through a *cloud* of flying, buzzing beasts. But Mom still won't do anything about them. She says they have as much right to the space as we do.

I pointed out that they aren't paying rent, and then Mom pointed out that neither am I.

Point: Mom.

But I have this creeping feeling like there might be something else in the house too. Something even worse. I kind of don't want to say it aloud (or even put it in writing) because it freaks me out, but I think there might be . . . . . . (((((spiders))))) in here. Oh God, pretend I didn't say that. I don't even want to think about it.

Getting really sick of living without furniture. But let's end this on a positive note: the movers will be here soon with all our stuff!

So, episode 3 of Paige's Humiliating Life. I thought nothing could be worse than everyone in school shunning me for no reason, but it turns out something is. The Weird Girl (you know what I mean, every school has one) wants to be my friend.

Seriously awkward. This girl—Chloe, I think?—dresses all in black and camo, and wears super heavy eye makeup. And her hair! Well, her hair is just ludicrous. Like, dyed black with a pink streak, but not a normal streak—it's *leopard* print. Is that not a cry for help? And obviously everyone else agrees, because no one ever talks to her, and she never talks to anyone either. Except me!

I now have that honor, since she came up to me at lunch and started asking me all kinds of creepy questions. Everyone else here (back when they were speaking to me) wanted to know about California and the movie business and all that. This girl just asks me about my new house. I'm like—this is *your* town, and the house has been sitting here for at least one hundred years. You probably know more about it than I do! Okay, I didn't say that, because I'm not a complete jerk. But I thought it.

How did I sink so low? What pathetic stench am I unwittingly giving off that makes this girl think I am an appropriate friend match for her? Although I guess she's right. Given the current situation, it's not like I'm going to do any better.

A part of me wants to blow her off in hopes that I can claw my way back into a respectable friend group at some point. But another part is like, eh, who cares? I've done the whole popular girl thing before, and it's not like it brought me a ton of happiness. Maybe I should experiment with being a weirdo outcast. I don't have much to lose, at this point.

(Drawing the line at leopard print hair, though.)

FRIDAY, JANUARY 16, 11:20 P.M.

I'm going to kill that little jerk.

The movers finally came with all our stuff (thank God!) and I was so happy and excited to see my bed and all my stuff again, you wouldn't believe. And I was trying to help out, carrying this big box full of lamps and picture frames and stuff, when Logan comes up and is like, "Hey Paige, look what I found." So I glance over at him and he rubs something sticky and gray on my sweater, and then he holds up his hands and they are covered with spider webbing.

So of course I drop the box and probably break forty things.

Uggggggh, trying so hard not to freak out. I mean, it's an old house, and old houses have cobwebs, right? It comes with the territory. But the spiders probably all died off a hundred years

ago. It totally doesn't mean there are legions of eight-legged monstrosities skittering in between the floorboards at night.

(oh, nice image, Paige. way to give yourself nightmares.)

deep breaths

It's okay. At least we have our stuff now, and the house is beginning to look like an actual place people live, and not like some hobo encampment. It is soooo nice to be able to curl up on a couch again, and cook real meals, and watch TV. Although the TV is acting weird—must be a problem with the cable hookup. I'll talk to Mom about it.

SUNDAY, JANUARY 18, 11:03 P.M.

Saw Weird Girl (Chloe) walk past my house twice this weekend, and stare up into the windows. Why is she so weird! I think I officially have a stalker.

MONDAY, JANUARY 19, 4:32 P.M.

Okay, I did it. I talked to Chloe after school today and it was okay. Don't get me wrong, this isn't some Lifetime movie where it turns out that the weird girl is nice and normal and just in need of a little kindness. She's *real weird*. But at least she's interesting.

For example, here's an actual conversational exchange we had today, on my walk home:

[Chloe lights a cigarette.]

Me: You smoke? Don't you know how bad it is for you?

Chloe: People say that. But it's only true if you think death is something to be avoided, rather than embraced.

Me: [. . .]

Then she goes back to asking me about the house. She's all, "So, what's it like?" What does that even mean? But she clarifies: "Is it really haunted?" And I think, ohhhh yeah, I should have seen that coming. Of course death-obsessed gothy girl wants to know if my creepy old house is haunted. Obvi.

So I roll my eyes, but she doesn't let it go. She's like, "Really? Nothing? No strange sounds, or lights flickering on and off, or random cold spots?" At that, I had to laugh. I explained to her that it's hard to find cold spots when the whole house is a freaking refrigerator. As for the noises . . . at first I was going to brush it off, but then I remembered the buzzing sound in Logan's room. So I mention that to her—how sometimes I can feel it in my teeth, and I'm not even sure if it's a sound or a feeling or what, but no one else seems bothered by it.

Her comment: "Wow, intense."

So I'm like, no, it's weird, but it's not supernatural, okay? Why would you even think that?

Chloe shrugs. "Maybe because of all the dead bodies."

So now there's that.

And she's like, the landlady didn't tell you? Back when this town was first founded, this house used to be the hospital. The basement was the morgue.

I admit, I might have gotten a few goose bumps. But I was pretty sure she was screwing with me, because I have been all up and down that house, and I never saw a basement. I tell her this, but Chloe gives me a weird look.

"Of course there's a basement," she says. "You can tell even from looking at the outside." We're half a block away from my house at that point, so she could show me. "See? There are little windows all along the bottom. There's got to be something down there."

And what do you know, she's right. I'd never even noticed.

That's when I remembered something slightly weird. There's

this random door in a kind of an out-of-the-way place right next to the kitchen. Or rather, there *was* a door. You have to look carefully, because it doesn't have a handle or anything. In fact, it's really just a doorway that has been walled up. I would never have noticed it at all if Mom hadn't been trying to hang a picture there and discovered that there was brick behind the plaster instead of wood like the other walls.

As I tell Chloe this, she raises her eyebrows as if this somehow constitutes proof that my house is haunted. Which it does not.

Except . . . when Chloe asked about funny noises in the house, there was one I didn't mention. In fact, I didn't even mention it here, I guess because I didn't want to admit it even to myself. But there's something about Chloe—weird as she is, she makes it feel sort of okay to admit that there is weird stuff in the world.

So I told her: One night last week I had fallen asleep on the couch downstairs and didn't wake up until after midnight. As I was tiptoeing up to bed, the wind died down just as I was passing in front of that walled-up door, and . . . I heard something. Chloe didn't say anything, she just raised her eyebrows in that way she does, as if inviting me to go on. It's hard to resist those eyebrows.

"Okay, this is going to sound crazy, but . . . it sounded like voices."

Chloe's expression didn't even change. It was as if she had been expecting this all along. "What were they saying?"

"I don't know, I couldn't make it out. And I'm not even totally sure it *was* voices. I'm not even sure it was anything at all, or if it's just my imagination playing tricks on me. I didn't exactly stick around to find out."

Chloe gazed at the house thoughtfully, her skirt whipping

around her legs as the wind blew in over those hills.

"Well, what do you think?" I said at last, trying to strike the right tone between serious and sarcastic. "Definitely haunted?"

"I don't know," she said. "I've heard things about this place all my life, but I've never been inside."

"Oh. Do you want to come in? But it usually seems pretty okay during the day. I mean . . . except for the gross cloud of flies hanging out in the entryway."

"Flies? In the middle of winter?"

I shrugged. Good thing the only person speaking to me is deeply weird, because I'm pretty sure any normal person would have freaked out when I announced that my house has an insect infestation. Chloe just raised her eyebrows slightly.

"Do you think I could stay overnight?" she said. "This weekend, I mean."

So, yup. That's the story of how I invited the Weird Girl over to my house for an awesome haunted house slumber party. Hope all my new zombie friends can make it!

WEDNESDAY, JANUARY 21, 11:05 P.M.

I am 300 percent done with Mom's stupid "the universe is a breathing organism" crap, and "we have to be stewards of the earth" and "every living thing is sacred," and yeah yeah that's all really beautiful but come on. We have to have some exceptions. We have to have an exception for spiders.

Because yes, we have spiders. I don't know how I didn't see before—some kind of mental block maybe? I think I just *so* didn't want to see them, didn't want to know, that I shut them out of my mind and out of my perception. But ever since Logan's little stunt with the cobweb, I have been seeing webs in every corner of the house. And they aren't always empty.

I thought I could handle it, I really tried to be stoic, but today I was sitting at my desk typing and one crawled over my *hand*. All those impossible little legs scurrying across my skin as if it was heading somewhere vitally important and I happened to be in its way.

So I may have screamed. I didn't even realize I was doing it until Mom came running into my room, obviously convinced I had broken a leg or been bitten by a raccoon or something. And she went into serious Mom mode and was all, "Paige, what happened, show me where it hurts, do I need to call an ambulance." Of course then I started crying and I pointed to the spider and . . . that's when she gave me the look.

The look that says, "You're kidding, right?" Where she sets her chin, and her lips make a thin line, and she just looks like she can't even believe I'm her daughter.

And I feel like the most worthless person in the world. But just . . . she doesn't get it. She thinks I'm being unreasonable, or unkind even. I can see the disappointment in her eyes when we talk about it, like she can't believe she produced someone so different from her, someone who doesn't see the world in the beautiful hippie earth mother way that she does. And I try to, I do. As much as I can. But spiders are . . . spiders are different.

This isn't just me being some tacky California girl and freaking out over every creepy crawly thing just to make myself seem feminine or cute or whatever. I'm pretty sure that what I have is a legit phobia. It's the legs—the way they coordinate in constant motion, all those pointy legs creeping and feeling, touching your flesh . . .

Then there's the way they crawl around where you can't see them. How they always crop up where you don't expect, dangling from a thread on the doorframe or in a cabinet. It's like they make safe, comfortable places suddenly threatening. Rationally, I know

31

the spiders around here won't hurt me, but they still trigger my urge to cleanse the house with fire.

And Mom *knows* this about me. I have been like this ever since I was a little kid. Since before Logan was born. I remember back in our old house I went up to the attic once to dig through the old boxes and see if I could find some toys or clothes to play dress-up or whatever, and there was a spider-web on one of the boxes—not even a spider, just a web!—and I basically lost my mind. Had nightmares for weeks. So it's not like this is news to her.

Anyway, she did calm me down some, and made me sit at the kitchen table for one of her "talks." Basically, she lectured me. All the Goddess's creatures, that whole bit. Tenderhearted Mom, cares more about the eight-legged freaks of the ~~animal insect~~ arachnid world than her own daughter! But she did at least promise that she and Logan would scour the whole house and sweep out all the cobwebs, and that should solve the problem.

And she did point out that spiders eat flies . . . and wasn't I just complaining about the flies?

Somehow that is cold comfort right now.

SATURDAY, JANUARY 24, 12:13 P.M.

Well, that was unexpected. And not entirely awful.

So, as arranged, Chloe came over to my house after school on Friday. It was definitely a little awkward at first, since we're not exactly friends. We don't really have anything in common except this house—Chloe because she's curious about it, and me because, well, I live here. So it's not like we had a lot to talk about. I kinda wished I could be like Logan and his new friends. All he has to do is show them to the video game consoles and they are set for the afternoon.

Luckily, Mom was there to smooth things over a bit, though that was also kind of embarrassing because she started doing her routine about how we come from this long line of mystics. Ugggggggh. The whole thing is ridiculous, and not something I believe in at ALL, and just makes Mom look either crazy or gullible. It's one thing to believe in respecting the earth and stuff, it's another to actually believe (contrary to ALL evidence) that you can control the universe with your mind.

I don't mind indulging her little hobby when it's just us, and it's been years since she did this in front of my friends because I told her how much I hated it, but I guess she decided that old rule didn't apply here, since Chloe was so clearly weird herself. I hadn't noticed before, but of course my mom remarked immediately that Chloe was wearing a pentagram around her neck. And it seems Chloe *was* interested, because while I sat there feeling awkward and trying not to roll my eyes, Chloe asked all kinds of questions about the family history, and Mom told all her stories that are either completely or largely made up, about my great-grandma being some kind of druid back in Ireland, and how there is this ancient energy that flows through our family line. Blah blah blah.

I finally got them to stop by inviting Chloe on a tour of the house. I knew she would go for that, since she has been curious about it for so long. Too bad there isn't all that much to see . . . It's not like we've got ghosts jumping out from behind corners. She didn't seem bored, though. She stood watching the flies swoop around for about five minutes. How's that for weird? And she asked a lot of questions about the history and structure of the house, most of which I couldn't answer.

I brought her into Logan's room because I wanted to see if she could hear the noise, but she had something else on her mind. "Where are the boarded-up windows?" she said before I could ask her about the buzzing. I had no idea what she was talking about, but she was like, "I can see from outside, some of the windows in the house look like they are boarded up."

I told her it must be a trick of the light or something, because no way would we leave any windows covered. Northern Idaho in the middle of winter is dark enough, and we're always trying to drag every ray of sunshine we can into the house. Then Logan came and kicked us out before I got a chance to draw her attention to the sound.

Anyway, that got us through the evening until Mom finally put the house to sleep and we wordlessly crept down to the secret door. It's funny but I was actually a little worried that we *wouldn't* hear anything. I think I was more nervous about looking like an idiot who imagined this whole thing than I was of actual ghosts. But sure enough, as we put our ears against the wall, there it was: a sound like muffled voices in conversation.

At first I felt a flutter of excitement. It was a relief to share this experience with someone, and not feel like I was completely crazy. But when I looked over at Chloe's shadowed face and saw her wide-eyed expression, I felt fear crawl back into my body and grip my guts.

"What do you think it means?" I whispered to her.

"I don't know. It seems crazy, but . . ." She pulled away from the door and stared at it, her expression set as if she was solving a puzzle. "The windows to the basement," she said. "Have you ever looked in them?"

Amazingly, that had not occurred to me, but now it seemed pretty obvious, and I led the way out of the house. A part of me knew I should be afraid, but excitement had taken over again, and I felt a lot more confident with Chloe by my side. We slipped down the front stairs and crept around the house toward where the windows were. I looked at Chloe, screwing up my courage, but she hesitated only a second before cupping her hands around her eyes and peering into the window. I followed suit.

After a few seconds I pulled away. "I can't make out anything," I said. "It's too dark." Chloe was still looking in the window, and she told me to look again. "Over there, toward the left," she said. "Do you see that?" I looked, and suddenly my fingers went numb with fear. Just faintly visible, off to one side, was a strange blue glow.

Without even thinking, I reached out and grabbed Chloe's hand. I realized right away that was a weird thing to do, what with us having just met and not particularly liking each other. But she didn't pull away, she just squeezed it back. My only thought at that point was to run back inside and hide under my covers, or wake up Mom and make her deal with it—whatever *it* was. But Chloe clearly had other things in mind. Dropping my hand, she took a few steps backward, as if to take in a view of the whole house in the moonlight. Again, she had that look on her face like she was in algebra class. "Paige," she said at last, "there's a door."

It took me a moment to even process what she meant. For a second I thought she was talking about the walled-up door inside. But then I followed her eyes and saw it: Tucked away around the back of the house and down a small flight of stairs was another door. A basement door.

I followed Chloe down the stairs and she tried the knob. The door gave way, groaning slightly as it opened. She gave me the briefest of looks over her shoulder, then stepped into the darkness. I took as deep a breath as my fear-constricted lungs would allow and joined her. At first, compared to the moonlit night outside, the basement seemed fathomlessly dark, but after a moment I noticed the same blue glow we had seen through the

windows. Chloe obviously saw it too and moved toward it, though I remained frozen in place. I was aware of her dark form blocking the glow as she progressed, until it became clear that she had made it to a doorway. I heard her give a strangled yelp, and that was all it took to free me from my paralysis. I screamed.

"What the hell?" I heard a voice through my scream, and it wasn't Chloe's. It was a guy's voice. "What are you doing in here? Calm down, Jesus, calm down."

A bright light came on, and I stopped screaming. Chloe's black-clad form came into view just in front of me as my eyes adjusted. And in front of her, slightly blocked by her, was a pale, lithe guy with a tangle of dark, curly hair flopped over his forehead. His eyes were dark and serious, and were framed by straight, sharp eyebrows. He was standing in his underwear. And he was staring at us.

"It's okay," said Chloe. "He's just a . . . I don't think he's a ghost."

"Pretty sure I'm not a ghost," the guy said. "Who are you?"

I didn't know what to say, and not because I was distracted by his incredible body. Definitely not that. "I live here," I tried.

"No," he said. "*I* live here. Look, can you hold on a sec? I want to have this conversation with pants on." He disappeared from my view a minute, during which time I realized that the blue glow we had seen must have come from a TV or a laptop in his bedroom. The boy came back wearing jeans and pulling a white T-shirt on over his head. He gave us both a once-over.

"You live upstairs, don't you?" he said to me. "I saw you when you moved in. And you . . . you're the weird girl who walks past this place three times a day and always stares at it."

"She's not weird," I said, feeling suddenly defensive on

Chloe's behalf. But Chloe apparently didn't need my support.

"Sure I am," she said. "It's kind of my thing."

At least she owns it. As the less weird member of our investigative team, I went ahead and introduced us both. He said his name was Raph (short for Raphael, I guess), and when he shook my hand, I may have trembled a little.

"Why did you scream?" said Raph. "You broke into *my* apartment, I should be screaming."

"Your door was unlocked," Chloe pointed out.

"Small-town Idaho. Who locks their doors? That's not an invitation to come wandering in at all hours of the night." A dark smile flickered across his face, his lip curling wickedly. "Small-town Idaho. You're lucky you didn't get shot for trespassing."

I couldn't help grinning back at him. "I'm sorry," I said. "I just, I didn't know anyone was living here. I didn't even realize this house had a basement until a few days ago. Why *are* you living here? Does anyone know?"

"I'm not a squatter, if that's what you're asking. I pay rent." Raph suddenly looked a little sheepish. "Most of the time, anyway. Sometimes. My mom owns this place. She's your landlady. I go to school," he said, nodding vaguely in the direction of the university. "The previous owners refinished this basement to be a mother-in-law apartment, and then my mom took over the house, and last year when I . . ." He combed a hand roughly through his hair. "Well, I decided to move off campus, and my mom said I could move in here. I help out around the place, fix stuff up when it needs it."

"There's a lot left to be fixed," I said, then blushed at my rudeness.

"You should have seen it before." He explained how the

place had stood empty for years, and was falling apart when she bought it. Raph had patched the roof and fixed up some of the plumbing, repaired some holes in the stairs. Guess he hadn't gotten around to insulation yet.

Chloe, ever on the prowl for macabre mysteries, asked why the house had been abandoned. "Did something bad happen here?"

"What, like a murder?" said Raph.

Chloe didn't say anything, but she gave me a meaningful look. Raph snorted in amusement. "Yeah, something bad happened here," he said. "Something bad happened everywhere. It's called the housing crisis. Ever pick up a newspaper? There was a family that lived here a while back, but the guy's store went out of business and they couldn't pay the mortgage and the bank foreclosed on them. The whole family moved in with his wife's parents."

"So the bank kicked them out, even though no one else wanted it?"

"It's what banks do," said Raph with a shrug. "Once it started to look run-down, the price went down, and my mom had the idea that she could turn it into a bed-and-breakfast. I didn't think she'd find anyone to rent such a big, weird old place in the meantime, but then you and your mom came along."

"It wasn't a morgue, then?" said Chloe.

"You've heard about that, huh? Yeah. There was a morgue down here in the basement once, back when it was the town's hospital. Is that why you guys thought it was haunted?" He looked between us, obviously amused. "Cute," he said. "But who would haunt a morgue? Think about it. A morgue is really just a way station. A place bodies rest a little while, between

40

when they died and when they get buried. If you were a wandering spirit, why would you hang around a morgue? You'd probably go to the place you died, or where something bad happened, or go find the person who wronged you. A morgue would be boring."

"You don't believe in ghosts," said Chloe, clearly disappointed.

Raph pressed his lips together. "There are no ghosts down here."

After that, Chloe and I left Raph alone and snuck back into the house and up to bed. It was very late by then, but we lay awake for some time, discussing what Raph had told us about the house. As for me, I found it kind of a relief to hear his stories. I was just as happy to hear that this house is not haunted, and it was just our overactive imaginations playing tricks on us. Chloe, though—I think she was actually disappointed. Maybe that's what it means to live in a small town. Life is so boring here, you start wishing for supernatural evil just to liven up the weekends a bit. Easy for her to say—she doesn't have to live here.

Eventually the spaces between our comments grew bigger, and I got the idea that Chloe was just about asleep. I closed my eyes, but before I drifted off, I put forward one last topic of conversation.

"Chloe?"

"Yeah?"

"Raph is kind of cute, I think."

"Um," said Chloe. "If by cute you mean devastatingly gorgeous, then yes. Kind of."

"But he's too old, right? I mean, how old do you think he is?"

Chloe considered. "Well, he's in college, obviously. And I

don't think he's a freshman . . . so he's probably like 20, at least."

"That's totally gross, right?"

"Gross and illegal," she confirmed. "Still . . . as ghosts go, Raph is definitely sexy."

Ha! Raph the sexy ghost. I like that.

MONDAY, JANUARY 26, 5:15 P.M.

The flies aren't gone, and neither are the spiders. If Mom's theory about spiders eating flies were correct, you'd think we'd see a diminution in one or the other. But this morning I saw five of the spiders standing together in the corner near my book bag, almost like they were plotting. And the flies just kept swooping around without a care in the world.

I'm really trying not to be such a baby about this stuff, but when I saw the spiders, I couldn't help it: I yelped. Logan came over to see what was wrong, and without even flinching, he just leaned down and scooped them up and tossed them outside. God, I have never been so grateful for my annoying little brother.

I felt a bit stupid as we walked to school together, and I was like, "You must think I'm pretty pathetic, huh?" But he was cool about it. He said he got used to dealing with gross stuff because of all the science experiments he does. It's not that he doesn't get creeped out, it's just that he's learned to control it. When you turn it into science, it stops being scary or gross, and just becomes data.

I asked him how I could turn the bugs into data, and he said to keep a notebook.

Ha. Is it really that simple?

TUESDAY, JANUARY 27, 4:10 P.M.

Spiders: 2 in the shower, 1 on the windowsill in my bedroom.
Flies: Too many to count, but maybe there are fewer? In any
case, the cloud seemed a little thinner this morning. So maybe
the spiders are pulling their weight around here after all?

Which really just begs the question: Which is better, spiders
or flies? Or let me rephrase that: Which do I loathe least? On
the face of it, this seems like an easy choice, because I have a
phobia of spiders, and no phobia of flies. I don't love flies, God
knows, but I'm not morbidly terrified of them either.

But the flies in this house . . . it's just that there are so *many*
of them. And they're so unavoidable. It's weird how they cluster
by the door. I can't see what is drawing them there. Wouldn't you
expect them to be near the food, or the trash? A drain, maybe?
But they insist on hanging out at the front door, which makes

every trip into or out of the house into a kind of horror show.

Spiders, on the other hand . . . well, at least they keep to themselves, mostly. You catch sight of them out of the corner of your eye, but you don't have to go swimming through vast hordes of them (ugh, that thought, why did I even think that?). But maybe it's not the spiders I see that worry me. For every spider you see, you know that there are at least a dozen more, hiding and waiting for you to go to sleep so they can walk on you and nip at you with those awful fangs . . .

shudder

I wonder if I could get the flies to eat the spiders? Or maybe they can both eat each other in a revolting free-for-all.

I'm not sure this is what Logan meant about thinking like a scientist.

Right. Moving on to cheerier subjects . . . we got our first real snowfall since I've been here! I woke up yesterday morning and my room was so much brighter than usual. I couldn't figure out why at first, but then I realized—the rolling brown hills outside my window weren't brown anymore. They were sparkling white! A big improvement, though it did make walking to school a bit of a pain.

Maybe after school tomorrow Logan and I can have that snowball fight we were promised.

Classes are fine, though I am still the school outcast. I guess one nice thing is that I pay a lot more attention in class now than I used to, when I was popular. Makes my homework easier.

Mom continues to be annoying. She got into this weird thing with me this evening when I was unpacking groceries. I was just trying to be helpful! But instead of thanking me, she started nagging about where I put stuff away. She was going on about how she bought two jars of pasta sauce and a whole crate of granola bars a few days ago, and now she can't find them anywhere in the kitchen. Like, how is that my fault? So she is micromanaging me about where to put all the stuff away, and I open a cabinet and there are SIX jars of pasta sauce. Ha! I have no idea why she bought so much pasta sauce, though. And apparently neither does she, since she swore she only bought two.

Then Logan was like, "It was probably ghosts." I laughed. What kind of ghosts mess with marinara? But Mom seemed to like the idea that we might be sharing the house with some "restless spirits." She is such a freak sometimes.

It's weirder from Logan. He's never shared in any of Mom's otherworldly interests. He's the scientist of the family, and pretty much always has been. I pointed this contradiction out to him, but he just shrugged. "Science means trusting the evidence of my senses." Whatever that means . . .

But Logan *has* been acting a little strange lately. He's been having trouble sleeping. I think it's because of the move and the divorce, not to mention the flies and the spiders and the wind screaming in the walls every night. But Mom seems a bit worried about him. I think mostly she feels guilty—under the circumstances, I guess it's easy for her to blame herself. No wonder she's a little absentminded . . . I guess I should cut her some slack.

Oh, but I did manage to ask her about Raph. I tried to be all, "So, uh, there's a dude living in our house, *jsyk*," but it turns out she did know, so then I felt dumb. Then she got on my case, and was like, "Paige, I *told* you the landlady's son lived downstairs, but you never listen to anything I say," blah blah. Why is it that the minute someone says, "You never listen to a word I say," I immediately start to tune them out?

Weirdly enough, Mom seems to be a total fan of Raph. Apparently she has been going down to his place now and then while I'm at school to bring him proper meals, because he's "much too thin." Hmm, that's one way of putting it. I would have gone with "lean" or "svelte" or maybe "outrageously gorgeous." Wait, does this mean Mom has been checking out Raph's

~~body?~~ Ew, I don't know why I even thought that. Don't think about that.

Anyway, she actually told me that he "seems like a nice boy" and that I should get to know him. Mom wants me to cozy up to a scorching hot college boy? Uh, okay, don't mind if I do.

SATURDAY, JANUARY 31, 3:15 P.M.

Sooo that was awkward.

The good news is, I figured out an excuse to go see Raph again. (Mom's permission or no, it felt weird to just knock on his door and be like, hi! wanna make out? ahem.) So yeah, I was trying to log on to the Internet to update this journal, but the stupid Wi-Fi has been crapping out lately. I don't know what is up with it. I reloaded a million times and kept getting different error messages. Rebooted the router, blah blah troubleshooting, but each time it would work for like a minute and then fritz out again. I need to bug Mom about it, along with the cable, which is still cutting in and out. (And doing odder stuff too—like the other day I was watching the end of a show, and instead of the next show coming on, the same episode started playing. I'm lazy, so I watched the whole thing again. But then it started playing again! And I know there was another show that was supposed to be on. The weird thing is, we don't even have a DVR.)

Anyway, I was checking the Wi-Fi network for the fiftieth time when it suddenly occurred to me that this situation might have a silver lining. There was this other network, very strong, called "The Morgue." It had to be Raph. Password protected, of course, but what better excuse to wander down and strike up a conversation? I know, pretty crafty!

So I head down there (after putting on some makeup and my best pair of jeans) and he answers the door in this pale blue T-shirt and was just looking . . . delicious, and I'm trying to be all supercool, like um, hey, my Wi-Fi is out, can I borrow your password? And he's like, yeah, if you want, but mine's been all over the place today too. Is it windy today? Sometimes the wind messes with the wires or something. So I'm like, mmm, yeah, wires. And he gives me the password and then we're, like, staring at each other.

So obviously I start babbling like an idiot, because I have nothing to say but I don't want to leave. So I say, "I hope I'm not bothering you. My mom told me to come down and ask. She really likes you or something, I guess." WTF am I even saying. So he's like, "Whaaa?" and I'm trying to think of a single flirty thing to say that doesn't make me look like an idiot, and I settle on, "Yeah, normally she is kind of uptight about me hanging out with older boys. Especially ones who . . ." and then right there I lose my nerve to say what was on my mind, so I just sort of peter out. I'm so cool.

Raph had been smiling pleasantly, adorably, through this whole performance, but right then, when I didn't end the sentence, he . . . I don't know, he looked serious all of a sudden. Or more than that, he looked . . . nervous? I kind of want to say haunted, but that's probably just because I have hauntings on the brain, thanks to Chloe. Anyway, I expected him to just smile and move on, maybe give me an "Okay, weird girl" look, but instead he gets this very intense look about him. I can see the muscles in his shoulders and arms tense up (not that I was checking out his body! okay, I was), and he's like, "Ones who what?"

Now I *really* don't want to say what I was thinking, except whatever *he's* thinking is apparently even worse, so I kind of have to. So even though I am feeling entirely flustered and awkward and embarrassed, I try to sound nonchalant as I say, "Ones who look like you." And then obviously blush like a dork.

But it wasn't allll bad because it brought the smile back to his face, and his shoulders relaxed, and then he looked down and ran a hand through those amazing curls and omg but HE WAS BLUSHING TOO. And it was pretty much the cutest thing I have ever seen. "Oh," he said. "Um . . . thanks."

And right then I was probably the happiest person in the world.

Yeah, that didn't last.

"I think I know why your mom is cool with us hanging out," he said, still looking all sweet and bashful and incredible. And I'm like, mmmm? And he says, "Probably because I told her I'm gay."

I know. I know. What is my life even.

But the best part is my brilliant response is to be like, "Oh. OH. Oh. So . . . wait. Are you? Gay?"

"No," says Raph, "I just told her that for shits and giggles."

"Oh," I say, and AGAIN my brain starts reeling before finally he figures out that I am a moron and need sarcasm explained to me.

"Paige," he says. "Yes. I'm gay. So your mom doesn't need to worry. And neither do you."

Hahaha FML. Ferreal.

SUNDAY, FEBRUARY 1, 10:28 A.M.

Flies: About the same, I think. No more or less. Except they seem . . . bigger, somehow. Maybe they have taken my suggestion after all and started to eat the spiders?
Spiders: 4 in the shower, 6 in my bedroom, 1 in my bed.

The less said about that the better.

Moving on. This is weird. Mom was freaking out last night (but not over spiders, which any reasonable person would freak out over) because she couldn't find her striped sweater. Not just any sweater, her *favorite* striped sweater. Which she suddenly needed to attend some department function. As if those eco-geeks care what anyone wears, as long as it's made from hemp.

Anyway, she came into my room and accused me of stealing her sweater. Unfair! Okay, yes, I have borrowed it on a few occasions. True. But in my defense, it looks better on me than on her. And anyway, I didn't take it! It's not like I've got anyone to impress here in Idaho—not even eco-geeks. Well, I guess there's Raph, but . . . yeah, it would have to be a pretty magical sweater to turn him straight, so. Point is, I did not take her sweater. Swear to God.

And I told Mom this, but she didn't believe me, so she opened up my closet to look for it, and in very dramatic fashion she turns around, holding up the missing sweater like she's Sherlock Holmes or something.

And that's weird, because I swear I have not even seen that sweater in months. But what's even weirder is that I notice over her shoulder . . . there are three other sweaters. Three other striped sweaters. That are totally identical to the one in her hands.

I pointed this out to Mom, and she agreed that it was weird, but idk, she deals with this stuff better than I do. Because while my whole body went cold and clammy, she just laughed. "Guess our astral roommates were a little bored tonight," she says in a too-loud voice, as if she figures they are listening. And I just cannot deal with that. I'm like, MOM. This isn't funny, this is seriously freaky. Isn't it?

But all she says is, someone just gave you free clothes, honey. Are you really going to complain?

Point: Mom.

WEDNESDAY, FEBRUARY 4, 5:20 P.M.

Flies: Big
Spiders: 16 since my last entry. I think.

I might have missed a few. I've been keeping track of them on a sticky note next to my computer, but that mostly only works for the ones I see in my room, or else I have to remember them until I get back to my room. You would think a person like me would have no trouble remembering seeing a spider, but sometimes other events do push them out of my head.

For example, it snowed again. A lot this time, so it's really deep. It's pretty when it falls, but I am getting a little sick of dealing with it on the ground. Guess I shouldn't complain too much, though, because when I got home, Raph was shoveling our porch and front walk. Glad I don't have to do that.

He looked really cold—he was all bundled up, with only his

eyes and the tip of his nose visible, and his nose was pink—so I asked if he wanted to come inside for some hot chocolate. He pulled the scarf down to uncover his mouth.

"Inside," he repeated. "Your place?" Like, duh. He looked up at the house, then back at me without answering. I sighed a little.

"It's just a warm drink," I said. "I get it, you're gay. Look, I don't bite."

At that, his cheeks blushed to match his nose. "It's not that," he said, "it's . . ." He broke off, huffing white vapor as he got his breath back from shoveling. "I used to spend a lot of time alone in that house," he said at last. "It . . . kind of got to me. The basement feels okay, but . . ."

"Really?" I said. "Not you, too. Am I the only person not convinced this place is haunted?"

"You mean Chloe?" he says. And I explain no, not just Chloe—Mom and Logan are always saying it too. And this, I guess unsurprisingly, does not seem to make him feel less uneasy. At last I roll my eyes and tell him I'll just bring it out to him. Which I do.

So then I'm handing him the chocolate and feeling like I have to make conversation now, so I mention that I don't think I've ever seen him out of his apartment before. He just nods at this, so I follow up with, "When do you go to class?"

Instead of answering, he takes a big gulp of hot chocolate and winds up choking on it. Adorably, but still pretty dorky. Anyway, he tells me he's taking a "light schedule this semester." So I ask what his major is, and he says history. "I mean, English. It was English, and then it was history. I guess." Which is kind of a weird answer.

"Oh," I say. "And now?"

"Now it's . . . I don't know. I guess not history anymore."

This conversation seems to be derailing fast, so I struggle to get it back on track. "So . . . English, then, or . . . ?"

"Maybe? We'll see. Technically I don't have a major." He takes a deep breath and looks out at the snow. "Technically I'm not a student."

This is odd and unexpected. I only just met the guy, and practically the very first thing he said to me was that he was a student at the university. And now he says he's not . . . Kind of awkward to catch someone in a lie within, like, the first hundred words they say to you. So now I don't know what to think. Or say. Luckily, he goes on.

"Medical leave of absence. Technically."

"Oh," I say, suddenly feeling like a huge jerk for mentally calling him a liar. "So you're like . . . sick? What's wrong with you?" Which is the most appallingly rude thing I could possibly have said, but he doesn't seem fazed. He just taps his forehead with one finger. "Oh God," I say, "brain tumor?"

He laughs. "No . . . I'm not dying, just crazy. Or so they tell me. Something happened last semester. I was working on this project with a professor, and . . . things got weird. Or I got weird. Or—I don't know. Anyway, it was decided that I needed some time off. To regroup."

I nodded sagely as if this all made complete sense, even though not any of it did. "What was the project?"

Raph just looked up at the house, as if something in the peeling gray paint was suddenly very fascinating. "I should get to that one of these days," he said. "It could cause problems down the road. If it's not repainted."

So I'm like . . . uh, okay. Why are we talking about paint now?

"You were about to tell me about the project?" I prompt him.

"I wasn't, actually." Raph gives me one of his long, intense looks, which—gay or not—still make me feel a little trembly. "You're pretty dense, aren't you?" he says. "When someone changes the subject like that, it's a way of saying 'I don't want to talk about it.' Got it?"

"Right," I say. "Sorry."

Guess someone's got a secret.

THURSDAY, FEBRUARY 5, 5:40 P.M.

Flies: About the same
Spiders: 8 since yesterday, I'm pretty sure.

I wonder if anyone has created an app to help people keep track of their spider infestations. If I could enter the sightings on my phone, I could keep my data more precisely, which I am told is important for science.

I suppose it wouldn't have to be specific to spiders. You could use the same app to keep track of all sorts of things that happen to scare the bejeezus out of you. Snakes. Rats. Clowns. Maybe there is someone out there right now writing an app to keep track of how many clowns he runs across every day, in hopes of calming his irrational fear of them. If so, I hope he makes it publicly available.

Not that it would do me much good these days. My phone is being a complete bastard.

God, why can't things just work? The Wi-Fi is sort of working now, since Mom called the ISP. I mean, the signal looks good, but there are weird dead spots all over the house, most particularly in my room! Which is really annoying. So basically if I want to be online at all, I have to hang out in the kitchen or one part of the living room. It's the strongest in Logan's room, which is weird because his room is, like, on the opposite side of the house from the router. I don't even know. And I hate going in there because of that buzzing noise.

But when I try to use my cell phone to go online, that's no better—my signal craps out at the randomest moments. Is this what it means to live in the middle of nowhere? It's fine when I'm at school, though. Raph says it has something to do with where the house is, but that makes no sense to me because we're at the top of a hill. Shouldn't that make the connections clearer? But then he says something about the wind.

Mom and Logan are even worse. If I bring it up with them, they just giggle that it's our "invisible roommates" messing with us. I can't tell if they really believe that, or if they just know it annoys the heck out of me. I'm leaning toward the second.

And the really annoying thing about the dead spots is that the minute I walk into a live spot, my phone gets flooded with all these messages that I obviously haven't been getting. I had three from Dad the other day, which I felt terrible about, because as mad as I am at him, I don't want him to think I'm giving him the silent treatment or whatever. Just because of some technological glitch. Missed a bunch of texts from Chloe, too. Oh, and I think I also got some actual friend requests but my stupid phone won't open them, so I can't even tell who they are from. So much for making any friends outside Chloe, since this is only going to confirm everyone's suspicion that I am stuck-up.

Then the other obnoxious thing is that when they do come through, I get a lot of double (or even triple or more) texts . . . so I'll feel like, woo, my phone is blowing up, but when I go to look at them, it's, like, five of the same text from Logan, asking if I know when Mom's going to be home. And sometimes the double text will come much later than the original text, like I'll get one every hour. Oh, and the latest nuisance is that I'll get texts from people but they show up blank. Or garbled, like maybe it's an autocorrect problem. But sometimes it looks like such gobbledygook that it's like they didn't even have auto-correct on. So I think it must be a virus or something. That reminds me, Chloe mentioned that some of my texts to her had come in garbled too. Gah, just what I need.

I don't know, should I try to download a virus scan thing? Or wipe the phone completely? Or make Mom call the service provider again?

Sorry, this is probably going to win some award for the most boring entry ever. Since I am the only person reading this, I will bestow the award myself. Hear ye hear ye, I hereby declare this journal entry an utter waste of electricity and pixels.

FRIDAY, FEBRUARY 6, 3:10 A.M.

Flies: About the same
Spiders: 8 since yesterday, I'm pretty sure.

I wonder if anyone has created an app to help people keep track of their spider infestations. If I could enter the sightings on my phone, I could keep my data more precisely, which I am told is important for science.

I suppose it wouldn't have to be specific to spiders. You could use the same app to keep track of all sorts of things that happen to scare the bejeezus out of you. Snakes. Rats. Clowns. Maybe there is someone out there right devil now writing an app to keep track of how many clowns he runs across every day, in hopes of calming his irrational fear of them. If so, I hope he makes it publicly available.

Not that it would do me much good these days. My phone is being a complete bastard.

God, why can't things just work? The Wi-Fi is sort of working now, since Mom called the ISP. I mean, the signal looks good, but there are weird dead spots all over the house, most particularly in my room! Which is really annoying. So everyone basically if I want to be online at all, I have to hang out in the kitchen or one part of the living room. It's the strongest in Logan's room, which is weird because his room is, like, on the opposite side of the house from the router. I don't even know. And I hate going in there because of that buzzing noise.

But when I try to use my cell phone to go online, that's no better—my signal craps out at the randomest moments. Is this what it means to live in the middle of nowhere? It's fine when I'm at school, though. Raph says it has something to do with where the house is, but that makes no sense to me because we're at the top of a hill. Shouldn't that make the connections clearer? But then he says something about the wind.

Mom and Logan are even worse. If I bring forgets it up with them, they just giggle that it's our "invisible roommates" messing with us. I can't tell if they really believe that, or if they just know it annoys the heck out of me. I'm leaning toward the second.

And the really annoying thing about the dead spots is that the minute I walk into a live spot, my phone gets flooded with all these messages that I obviously haven't been getting. I had three from Dad the other day, which I felt terrible about, because as mad as I am at him, I don't want him to think I'm giving him the silent treatment or whatever. Just because of some technological glitch. Missed a bunch of texts from Chloe, too. Oh, and I think I also got some actual friend requests but my stupid phone won't open them, so I can't even tell who they are from. So much for making any friends outside Chloe, since this is only going to confirm everyone's suspicion that I am stuck-up.

Then the other obnoxious thing is that when they do come through, I get a lot of double (or even triple or more) texts . . . so I'll feel like, woo, my phone is blowing up, but when I go to look at them, it's, like, five of the same stone text from Logan, asking if I know when Mom's going to be home. And sometimes the double text will come much later than the original text, like I'll get one every hour. Oh, and the latest nuisance is that I'll get texts from people but they show up blank. Or garbled, like maybe it's an embodied autocorrect problem. But sometimes it looks like such gobbledygook that it's like they didn't even have autocorrect on. So I think it must be a virus or something. That reminds me, Chloe mentioned that some of my texts to her had come in garbled too. Gah, just what I need.

I don't know, should I try to download a virus scan thing? Or wipe the phone completely? Or make Mom call the service provider again?

Sorry, this is probably going to win some award for the most boring entry ever. Since I am the only person reading this, I will bestow the award myself. Hear ye hear ye, I hereby declare this journal entry lies an utter waste of electricity and pixels.

SATURDAY, FEBRUARY 7, 9:17 A.M.

Huh, that's weird. I just realized my last entry posted twice. I must have hit the post button funny or . . . but it's weird because the time stamp is hours and hours later than the original post. How would that even happen?

Anyway, just logged on to record my bug tracking.

Flies: The cloud seems denser today.

Spiders: 10 this morning

WEDNESDAY, FEBRUARY 11, 3:22 A.M.

Woke up to the sound of screaming.

At first I thought it was me, waking myself up from a nightmare with my own shrieks. But even after I lay in bed a moment, letting my heart rate calm, I could still hear it. Feel it like it was coming from inside me, but my mouth was closed.

It's just the wind, I think. There's another massive storm raging outside, shards of lightning splitting the empty landscape outside my window, whirling gusts of snow billowing against a purple sky. And when the wind picks up, it pierces every crack in this old house and howls and moans like a dying animal.

And under it all I can still hear that buzzing from Logan's room. It's getting worse, like it's drilling in my head, making my teeth vibrate. It doesn't even feel like it's separate from the wind. Maybe it's because my head is still fogged with sleep, but somehow the sounds feel linked, or like one is a version of the other.

I guess while I'm up, I might as well tell the funny story of the missing packages. So a couple of days ago, Mom busted a taillight on the car while backing out of our driveway. I'm going to remember that next time she gives me a hard time during my driving lessons. Anyway, rather than trust an actual professional with the repair, Mom got it into her head that she could just order the new taillight off the Internet and install it herself. So she paid extra for the one-day shipping, but the package didn't come. And didn't come. And didn't come, so finally she sent a complaint, and they said they would send another one out right away. And that one didn't come either, so she sent another complaint, and they apologized again, etc. etc.

Well, the upshot is, yesterday we got SEVEN taillights delivered to our house. And guess what—every one of them is

Okay, that was weird. Logan just came into my room, and we had a seriously oddball conversation. I couldn't even tell if he was awake or asleep, to be honest . . . although he has never been a sleepwalker. Insomnia is his gig lately, which I knew from my mom, but I guess this was the first time I was up in the middle of the night to experience it firsthand.

Anyway, he came in and sat on my bed and stared at me. I was sitting up with my laptop in my lap. And I was like, Logan? What are you doing? Go back to bed. He didn't say anything, but he sort of shrugged, so I think he heard me. Normally if he comes into my room, I tell him to scat in no uncertain terms, but he seemed so weird that I tried to be gentle . . . I told him he'd feel better if he went back into his room and got into bed. And then he goes, "I can't go back in there." And I'm like, why? And he's like, "The wall." And I'm like . . . wha?

"There are words in the walls. Or some kind of . . ." He looks around. "Your room doesn't have them."

So at this point I'm like, okay, the kid had a bad dream, thought he saw something scary in his room. Typical little kid stuff, though Logan isn't so little anymore—I don't think kids are supposed to be seeing monsters in the closet at his age. But hell, everyone in this household is on edge these days. So I'm like, "It's okay, Logan, I'll go back to your room with you and show you there is nothing wrong with your walls. It's probably just a shadow or a water stain or something."

He seems cool with this, so I take his hand and we go over to his room and I look around quickly and I'm like, "See? No one in here. Perfectly safe." And he doesn't say anything, he just . . . points. Toward the wall, which is different from mine, he has wood paneling in his room, where I just have plaster. So I walk over to where he's pointing and I'm like, whatever, these are just normal swirls in the wood, but then I get closer and . . . it's weird, because suddenly I can see it. It really does look like there is some kind of writing in the paneling.

But if it's writing, I should be able to read it, right? But I can't, exactly. It's like, if I glance at it askew, I get a sense that there are words there, but when I look at it directly, they lose all definition and it doesn't even look like proper letters. Although maybe in another language? Like Arabic or something? Or symbols of some kind?

But what it's really like is dream writing—you know, when you're dreaming and you pick up a book or look at a sign and you know there are words there, but they swirl and run together and writhe on the page and you can't make them resolve into actual language? I used to always use this trick to tell if I was dreaming—if I thought I was, I'd pick up a newspaper or something, and if I couldn't read it, I knew I was in a dream.

But this isn't a dream. Right?

I couldn't send Logan to bed after that. Hell, I wouldn't sleep in his room after that (not to mention the annoying buzzing noise in there that always makes my head ring). Instead I asked him if he wanted to watch TV, and I took him downstairs to the living room and put on a movie for him. And I got my laptop and now I am keeping him company, or maybe he is keeping me company, because I sure as hell am not going to sleep anymore tonight.

Oh, I guess I never finished my story from before. So yeah, the punchline is that all seven of the stupid taillights that came are for the wrong side of the car. That seemed funnier an hour ago.

FRIDAY, FEBRUARY 13, 5:04 P.M.

Flies: Bigger? I'm not sure. Qualitative measures are a bit hard to judge, especially when I don't have the specimens side by side. I wonder if I should start capturing and storing flies, for purposes of comparison.

Wow, I really am losing it. Who knew there was such a thin line between "scientist" and "batshit insane"?

Spiders: 10 since last time

I told Chloe about the words in the wall and she was like, whoa, that's so cool! You have to show me. So I guess that's a thing.

I was annoyed at first, because I'm really worried about Logan and this seemed like a pretty traumatic experience for him. I mean, it's not a joke. And then, hell, I'll admit it, I was pretty freaked out too—I don't even have to sleep in that room, but I see those words behind my eyelids as I'm drifting off to sleep most nights now, and let me tell you, it's unsettling.

So I was kind of pissy with Chloe about it at first, and not interested in hearing her stupid goth enthusiasm for everything spooky, as if this was some Halloween theme park run by the local church or something, rather than our actual lives. But even though I was kind of moody about it, she kept pressing for more details and descriptions, and wouldn't let it drop, and . . . well, I guess her enthusiasm is kind of infectious, because after a while I got into telling the story, and I got excited about bringing her home to show her. She was telling me about these websites where people post pictures of this kind of thing—messages from the beyond or whatever—and she said most of them are either really dumb looking, like you can't see anything at all, or else they are so obviously edited by some troll just looking for attention. And I wound up kind of excited about sharing this weird experience with the world.

On the one hand . . . I don't really want anything in my life to support the idea that I live in a haunted house. I just don't need that. But on the other . . . well, it seems less scary and more fun when a whole bunch of other people are invested in the question too.

I just hope I can sell Logan on the idea.

Thursday, February 19, 11:16 P.M.

Flies: About the same
Spiders: 9

Is Logan's advice working? It's definitely not making the flies and spiders go away. Is it helping me deal with them? I don't know. A little, I guess. Counting them at least gives me something to occupy my mind when I start to freak out.

I've been sweeping out the spiderwebs whenever I see them, but it doesn't seem to do any good. And I'm not sure everyone else in the house is totally supportive of my efforts.

I get that Logan's not freaked out by spiders like I am, which is good for him, I wouldn't wish this annoying phobia on anyone, but . . . sometimes I think his interest is more than purely scientific.

Like lately, I don't know if I'm just imagining it, or if my mind is playing tricks on me, but it seems like sometimes I catch him . . . *playing* with the spiders. I don't know, I've never seen anything, not really, and it feels crazy just to say it. It's just that sometimes I'll go in his room and he'll be really quick to usher me out of it. Which is totally normal little brother behavior, and there could be a billion normal things he is hiding in there from me.

But then there were a few times when I saw him, late at night or early in the morning, sitting on the stairs, or on the landing where the stairs turn, and sort of . . . poking around something in a corner. Why would he do that? And when I asked him, he wouldn't talk about it. But I know there are some holes in that area where the floorboards don't quite meet, and that's one of the places where I know I've seen spiderwebs that come back even after you've swept them away.

And a couple times, out of the corner of my eye, I saw Logan doing something weird with his hands, and I don't know if I'm just hypersensitive or something, but it looked like he was letting them crawl on him, like, deliberately. And just sort of watching them with this interested look on his face.

But that can't be. God, where do I come up with this stuff? It's like I'm actively trying to freak myself out. If I can get the damn Internet to work, I'm going to watch a bunch of kitten videos and try to get this horrible thought out of my head.

SATURDAY, FEBRUARY 21, 11:52 A.M.

Ugh, I am trying to get in touch with Chloe to figure out when she can come over to look at Logan's walls, but my texts keep disappearing into the ether. Or else they show up garbled beyond deciphering—just nonsense words and key mash. Though she told me the other day that last week she got six messages from me over the course of an hour and they all said "blood on the tail of the pig." Haha, what? Where the hell did that come from? Mom would say the universe is trying to tell me something, but damned if I know what.

MONDAY, FEBRUARY 23, 3:32 A.M.

It is impossible to get a decent night's sleep in this house!

I guess I shouldn't complain, since Logan clearly has it worse than I do. Though between being an insomniac and being woken up from a lovely dream in the middle of the night by your insomniac little brother, I'm not sure which is preferable.

In any case, it was right around 3 a.m. that I woke up to Logan messing around in my room, going through my closet and drawers. I asked him what the hell he was doing, and he just mumbled something. I asked him again and he turned around with a fierce expression, just visible in the moonlight streaming in through the window.

"I'm looking for my game."

For a minute I couldn't even answer this, it was so absurd. His video game? That had to be what he meant, but . . . in the

middle of the night? And what would it be doing in my room? It didn't make any sense. But he didn't seem concerned with logic.

"I've looked everywhere else and I can't find it. It has to be somewhere. Help me look."

I got out of bed and crossed the room to him, planning to grab him by the arm and haul him back to his bed, but before I reached him, he gasped in amazement and I stopped short.

"What is it?" I said.

He pulled his hand out of the trunk he'd been rifling in, a trunk I hadn't even opened since a day or two after the movers brought it, and in his hand was a video game disk.

Surprise was written across his face, and his hand trembled a little, but he was smiling triumphantly none the less. "Yes," he exclaimed. "I found it! I knew it had to be somewhere." Then, as he took a closer look, his expression shifted to confusion, and he dove back into the trunk, muttering to himself about how that "couldn't be right."

As I watched, he pulled another disk out of the trunk, then another, and another. Finally he sat back on his heels and looked at me. "Monster Party," he said. "All Monster Party. All I want is my Polybius disk, and instead I find four copies of a game I haven't played in five years."

I stared at him mutely. I couldn't figure out why any of his games would be in my trunk, let alone four copies of one.

Suddenly his face screwed up with rage, and he hurled the games across the room, where they smashed into the wall and fell to the floor.

"What the hell," was all I could say.

Logan got up and left the room.

SUNDAY, MARCH 1, 5:04 P.M.

I can't believe we just got another six inches of snow, on top of the three inches we got last week. It's March! Isn't it supposed to be spring? Oh right: Idaho. It's probably never spring here.

It is really pretty, especially the view out my windows over the rolling white hills, but enough is enough already. I'm tired of feeling like a captive in this house. I want to go running again. I want the walk to school not to leave me sore and exhausted. I want it to stop being so damn cold all the time. I want to wear pretty floral dresses and sandals, not sweaters and boots.

Hold on, Logan is freaking out about something. I better see.

Heeeeeeeey, school got called off tomorrow! Logan just told me they announced it on TV. I've heard about snow days, but I don't think it had occurred to me as a thing that might happen

in my life. Okay, I guess I don't mind if winter sticks around a *little* longer.

Nice to see Logan in a good mood, too. And not acting . . . however you'd describe what he's been like recently. He's been all right lately. Maybe it's out of his system.

WEDNESDAY, MARCH 4, 7:30 P.M.

Chloe's over right now. She and Logan are blathering on about occult messages, so I thought I'd update my journal.

She came over tonight for dinner, which was awkward to begin with because Mom didn't remember even though I reminded her this morning. Not that she minded, but it seemed to throw her off her game a bit—inasmuch as Mom has a "game" at the best of times, which is not much. So she was futzing around in the kitchen, going through her cookbooks and opening and shutting the cabinets absentmindedly as she asked us our plans for the evening. And Chloe immediately starts telling her about the words in the walls, I guess assuming Logan and I had told her about it. Which we had not.

So Chloe's babbling on about this website and how we're going to send in some photos, and Mom turns around with this concerned expression, and she's like, are you sure this is a good idea?

And I try to signal to Chloe to let it drop, but she is so excited she starts describing the website to Mom, and meanwhile Mom's concern-face is deepening steadily. And finally she sighs and she's like, "I really don't think this is a good idea."

So I'm like, "Aren't you always saying that the spirit world is nothing to be afraid of?"

And she has to concede this, but she still looks unthrilled. And as she goes back to opening and closing all the cupboards, she lectures us a little vaguely about being respectful toward the dead, and not exploiting the energy in the house for our own personal glory, etc. To which I snark, "If you think having a pic posted on a website equals glory, you might want to recalibrate your measures of fame a little."

I was just kidding around, but right then she slams the cupboard and turns around and shouts, "I don't believe it!"

Which, like . . . it's not like I've never seen my mom mad before, but it's definitely a rare occurrence, given how committed she is to peace and patience and whatnot. So I definitely jumped. And I was about to defend my little joke when she starts going off about these vegetables. I guess she had gone to the co-op (basically, the fancy, pricey grocery store) yesterday and gotten all these fresh veggies and health foods and was planning to make some elaborate meal tonight, but now she can't find any of the stuff she bought in the fridge or the pantry.

So then Logan breaks the tension by saying, "Maybe it's the ghosts. They really want us to have spaghetti tonight. We've still got plenty of that, right?" And Mom kind of sighs and can't help grinning a bit, and she does make spaghetti, because what else is she going to do?

But after dinner she makes me help her with the dishes while Chloe chats with Logan, and she's wearing her concerned-mom face again. And she's like, Paige, is there something you'd like to talk about?

And I just . . . I got kind of teary, because there is so much I want to talk about. So much we never talk about. About Dad, and what's happening with Logan, and this house, and all the weird stuff that's been going on . . . But I don't even know where to begin, so I don't say anything, and then Mom starts in on my *food intake* of all things. It was completely out of left field, except she was bulimic for a while in her 20s, when she was in the movies and there was all this pressure on her to be thin and gorgeous. And she's always worried that I would pick that up at some point, but like . . . I'm not in the movies. And it's not like anyone is looking at my body here in Idaho, where everyone has to wear 17 layers all winter or they'll freeze to death. It's just . . . yeah, I used to diet sometimes back in LA, but lately, with everything else on my mind, it's not something I've been thinking about.

But I guess she read some mom-pamphlet somewhere that said if food goes missing from your house, your teenage daughter probably has an eating disorder. I think they probably had cupcakes and cheese curls in mind rather than bulgur and quinoa. Why would I hoard that? But in any case, I'm not hoarding anything. And I'm trying to convince her of this, but everything I say comes out sounding defensive, which just makes her look even more concerned, until I feel like I'm at my wits' end.

So finally, just to move the conversation forward, I'm like, have you ever considered it might be Logan? And she rolls her eyes, like Logan has an eating disorder? Yeah, right. So I'm like, well, maybe not an ED exactly, but . . . I've seen all these stories about people who eat when they sleepwalk. Sleep-eat. And Mom points out that Logan doesn't sleepwalk, and I'm like, yeah, but . . . you have to admit, he's been acting weird. And he's up for so many hours when no one else is. What does he do with all that time?

And Mom says, "You think he's making quinoa tabouleh salad?" She has a point. This kid only just learned how to use a can opener so he can microwave himself some ravioli. He's not a genius in the kitchen, and he's definitely no health food guru. And it would be really out of character for him to clean all the plates and pots and counters and everything when he was done . . . but maybe his insomniac self is a neat freak, I don't know.

Anyway, she clearly doesn't believe my story, and is still acting all suspicious toward me and keeps prodding me about where the food went, like she's convinced I'm lying to her and she's not going to leave me alone until she gets to the bottom of this. And that's when I'm like, well, you're the one who had seven wrong taillights sent to the house. Are you going to blame me and Logan for that, too?

And Mom looks deeply annoyed at that jibe, and she's about to respond when we're both distracted by a noise behind us. And we step out of the pantry to look, and there's a big bag of vegetables in the middle of the kitchen floor.

Mom goes over to the bag and starts pulling stuff out of it— peppers, zucchini, onions. And she's got this look on her face of, like, complete bewilderment. I think something really shifted for her in that moment. All the other stuff that has been happening . . . she called it spirits, but she didn't *really* believe it. But sitting there with those onions in her hands, it's like she couldn't deny it any longer.

She raised her eyes toward the ceiling. "Thank you?" she said. But she sounded a little unsure of herself.

Chloe and Logan are totally absorbed in the wall writing now, but I'm still a little weirded out by what happened with the veggies.

I asked Logan if he could explain it according to scientific principles, and he says, "Well . . . all matter is made up of atoms, right? And atoms are made up of subatomic particles. And subatomic particles are constantly moving. Normally, their movement is so tiny and so random that all the different movements of all the subatomic particles cancel each other out. But if, by random chance, all the particles suddenly moved in the same direction, that could make the vegetables move on their own. Scientifically."

Um, what? Am I supposed to believe that?

Logan says no, not really. Which is why he is going with an

alternate explanation. But somehow I like that alternative even less.

At least that annoying noise in Logan's room isn't bothering me as much as usual. Maybe having Chloe here, and the two of them laughing and talking, is drowning it out. I can still feel it through my body like when you're leaning against a car with the engine running, but it's not noisy, and it's not uncomfortable.

Anyway, Chloe and Logan have been talking and taking photos for ages now, but Chloe isn't happy with how any of them are turning out. I guess she wants to try it with the lights off and her flash, so I'll end this now.

WEDNESDAY, MARCH 4, 11: 36 P.M.

I never want to talk to Chloe again. He's just a kid! And now—

I need to calm down. He's going to be okay. The doctors are saying he's fine. But God, I don't ever want to see something like that again. One minute Chloe was snapping some cell phone photos in the darkness of his room. Then all of a sudden I started feeling that buzzing build up again . . . It started in my stomach muscles, then spread into my chest and my head, and this time it didn't sound like someone screaming, it sounded like a dozen people screaming . . . or wailing . . . but not human at the same time. Mechanical, somehow.

I shut my eyes tight because the vibrations were making me queasy, and then I heard a loud thump, and Chloe was yelling Logan's name. I opened my eyes in the darkness and felt for him while Chloe ran for the light switch. When the light came on,

Logan was on the floor, and he . . . he didn't look right at all. His limbs were stiff and extended, his muscles tensed, and he was shaking and drooling, with his eyes rolled so far back I could only see the whites.

I screamed for Mom, who came running, and the rest is kind of a blur of 911 calls and ambulances and stuff.

So now I am at the hospital updating on my phone, and Mom is meeting with the doctors and Logan is in some room strapped to all these wires and machines, and no one is really telling me anything, except not to worry, and that everything is going to be fine.

I want to believe them, but this doesn't feel fine.

SATURDAY, MARCH 7, 9:25 A.M.

I've fallen behind on my Science Duties.

Flies: Annoying

Spiders: A dozen or so

God, what a week this has been. Chloe feels terrible, of course. The doctors agree that Logan's seizure was probably brought on by the flash from her camera phone, and for a while I was furious with her for that, but . . . how could she have known? It's not like Logan had any history of this sort of thing. It could have just as easily been me with the camera in my hand.

The weird thing is, the doctors aren't even sure it was really a seizure. I don't know, I don't totally understand, but they ran their tests, the EEG or whatever, and they say there's no evidence of abnormal brain activity. But how can that be?

The neurologist said it was a "pseudo-seizure," and that from the outside they look indistinguishable from regular seizures, and the victim can't tell the difference either. They're not intentional or anything, but she said they could be caused by stress or anxiety. She acted like this was good news, and of course it's good that there's nothing biologically wrong with Logan's brain, but I don't think Mom was too happy to hear that it's stress-related, either.

Anyway, the neurologist referred Logan to a new doctor now. A shrink, Dr. Louisa Clyde, who says that it's probably a side effect of the ADHD drugs he's on. Which she says also probably explains the insomnia . . . which I guess makes sense. Those pills are basically speed, aren't they? No wonder he can't sleep.

In any case, they taught us what to do if it happens again: roll him on his side, loosen his clothes, slip a pillow under his head. It's good not to feel so helpless, but I hope I never have to use this information. I don't want to see him like that again.

Dr. Clyde's big idea is that we should just take him off the pills for a while and see if he stabilizes a bit. Lack of sleep is also a pretty common trigger for seizures . . . The doctors were pretty shocked when me and Mom couldn't tell them when the last time Logan slept was. I mean, I think I always assumed that he slept *sometimes*. When I wasn't looking. When I was sleeping. But God, yeah . . . it's been a really long time since I *saw* him sleep. They said normally people with insomnia make it up somewhere. Naps during the day or whatever. The body's not designed to go completely without sleep for a long time. They actually seemed more concerned about that than the seizure.

Anyway, hopefully getting him off the medication will help him sleep, and stop the seizure thing from happening, and make him . . . okay again.

It's all really scary and upsetting, except . . . this is terrible to say, but a part of me was really glad to hear the thing about the medication. It was just such a relief to get an actual, like, scientific reason for some of the stuff that's been going on. I know the veggies in the kitchen story is silly and seems like a joke, but at the same time, how the hell does this stuff keep happening? All we can think to do is blame each other for each weird event, but none of it adds up, and it just makes us snipe at each other all the time. I'm sick of Mom not trusting me, and I'm sick of not trusting her or Logan. Not that I think they are deliberately messing with me, but it's upsetting to think that I can't trust them to be normal. To be sane. To not be moving stuff in the middle of the night or forgetting things or getting confused all the time.

For that matter, it's upsetting to not really be able to trust myself. I mean, what if I'm just as bad? What if I'm the one hiding video games and stealing sweaters and sending garbled text messages, and I just don't remember?

I don't like thinking about that.

I'm hoping, with this change, that everything will settle down for a bit.

TUESDAY, MARCH 10, 4:07 P.M.

I can't believe the weather today. Finally the snow melts, but instead of blue skies and warm spring breezes we get . . . WTF is this, anyway? A sandstorm, I guess. All I know is that it's impossible to walk down the street without getting buffeted by the wind, and no matter how tightly I tie back my hair, by the time I get to school, my cheeks hurt from where it has come loose and whipped me in the face.

And even worse is the sand—or maybe dust, or grit—that blows into town from those big empty fields and stings my eyes and crunches between my teeth no matter how snugly I wrap my scarf around my face. This can't be normal. There is a deep-seated evil in this place, I swear.

On a more positive note, I can see just a hint of green on the hills outside my window, though mostly the landscape still looks muddy and brown. Delightful.

SUNDAY, MARCH 15, 3:25 A.M.

I'm up in the middle of the night again. And I'm not alone.

Ugh, wasn't everything supposed to be better now?

I guess Dr. Clyde's new routine for Logan hasn't exactly kicked in yet. I woke up around 3 a.m. with strange sounds in my ears. Mixed in with my dream state it sounded almost like children playing, or maybe like fairy laughter . . . but eerie somehow. Anyway, I tried to ignore it and go back to sleep, but it kept annoying me, so finally I got up and followed the noise out to the hall. The whole house was dark, except for a blue glow coming from downstairs, and I was unavoidably reminded of the blue glow Chloe and I saw that first time we met Raph.

The sight of it gave me a chill at first, just remembering how frightened I had been that night. But then I reminded myself of how that turned out—not scary at all, right? And this must be the same thing, just the TV on in the middle of the night. Not scary.

So I went down the stairs and into the living room, and . . . well, I was right. In a sense. Logan was sitting in front of the TV, playing one of his video games. That was the music that had been haunting my dreams, of course. But I was wrong to think it wasn't scary. I don't know, I can't explain it. Logan was just so transfixed. But so what? Everyone looks transfixed when they're playing video games, right?

But this was different, somehow. More like that time he came into my room, and I couldn't quite tell if he was in a trance or what. It was like he wasn't even really playing the game—his thumbs were moving, but his brain didn't seem to be engaged.

So I was like, "Logan? Are you okay? Why don't you come to bed, honey?" But he just ignored me. It was creeping me out, for real. So finally I went over to him and sat behind him on the couch. My knee was touching his back, but he didn't react to it at all, so I laid a hand on his shoulder and tried to shake him gently. But he didn't . . . he didn't move the way a sleepwalking person would. He resisted me, like he was playing statue or something. Held himself perfectly still and straight, and didn't make any response to me at all.

So then I tried to be like, "How about we just finish this level, and then back to bed, okay?" And I figured I would watch along and give him tips, both to relate to him, and hopefully to get him to finish faster. But as I watched, I realized something. Logan . . . wasn't really playing. I mean, he was—his fingers were moving on the buttons, and they were affecting the stuff on the screen—but he kept dying like every minute or two. He hadn't gotten beyond level 1! And this is Logan—I've seen him play this game a million times. He's basically an expert. He could make it to level 9 in his sleep . . . at least that's what I would have said until tonight.

Because now, as I watched, he just kept dying, over and over and over. Misjudging a jump or meeting up with a bad guy or just running headlong off a cliff. He wasn't playing like himself at all. And each time, he would just go back and start again, as if nothing was wrong.

Eventually I left him and came back up to bed, but I sure as hell can't sleep now. How long is he going to be like this?

WEDNESDAY, MARCH 18, 4:56 P.M.

Flies: LOUD. Were they always this loud? bzz bzz bzz.

Spiders: 16ish

Is there really any point in me keeping track of the spiders? For every spider I see, I know there are loads that are invisible to me, so what exactly am I recording? (For Science!) How brave they are? How bold? How deeply they want to piss me off? I suppose the point was to give me something to do other than shriek and run from the house in terror every time I see one, and I guess it has worked, in that respect. But that makes me feel more like Logan is studying me for some kind of psych experiment, instead of me studying the spiders.

Knowing Logan, I guess that isn't all that implausible. If he winds up publishing his results in some medical journal, I hope he'll at least have the good taste to change my name.

Speaking of Logan, I told Mom about what happened the other night with him. She didn't really get it. She said if he couldn't sleep, it was better to get up and do something than just lie in bed. That's what all the experts say. I tried to explain to her how eerie the whole thing was, but she doesn't know enough about video games to really get it. Besides, I was holding back a bit, because I didn't want to freak her out. I got her to make another appointment with Dr. Clyde, so hopefully that will help at least.

I talked with her about some other stuff too. I don't know, I've been trying not to say anything to her, partly because I feel like she has enough on her mind, and also because I didn't want her to tease me or think I was being silly. Except that is totally not Mom. So maybe what I was really afraid of was that she would agree with me . . . and talking to her would just make it all the more real.

Well, I wasn't totally wrong. But it went really well, considering.

I was just like, Mom, I know we've kidded around about it a bunch, but do you seriously think this house might be, you know . . . haunted? And I was preparing mentally for her to either be like, "Paige, grow up," or on the other hand to be like, "Yes and demons have been speaking to me from the coffee-maker." Neither of which I wanted to hear.

But she was pretty cool about it. She basically said that yes, she believes there are spirits inhabiting the house, but no, she wouldn't call it a haunting. Which I know, that makes about zero sense, but I guess I know what she means. She said haunting is a negative term that people use because they are afraid of any "disembodied consciousness," so they want to name it and contain it. They'll call a house "haunted" to reassure themselves that the other houses are not.

But the truth is, the spirit world is all around us, all the time. Any time someone dies, they leave a little imprint of their consciousness on the world, and it continues to influence the living, though some people are more sensitive to it than others. This house—a lot of people have passed through it, and they have all left a little bit of themselves. Spiritually. But it's nothing to be afraid of.

She told me to think of them as, like, roommates. Some roommates are easy to get along with, some are a little harder, but everyone is basically good, so if you are patient and understanding, there is no reason we shouldn't all be able to get along.

I don't know. I don't believe in that stuff the way Mom does. At least I didn't . . . Maybe now I do. In any case, it was weirdly comforting. I didn't expect it to be, but what she was saying made more sense than anything else that's been going through my head lately.

Anyway, she gave me a big hug and asked me if I was feeling better, and I nodded, because I really was, but something about the hug and the way she was being so nice and momlike made my eyes tear up like a goon. So then she was like, Paige honey . . . would you feel better if I did a smudging?

And yeah, I know I don't believe in that stuff, and I have always made fun of Mom doing it. In fact, I remember now that she had planned to smudge the house the day we moved in, but Logan and I teased her so much about it that she let it drop. Maybe that was dumb.

Anyway, I half surprised myself by being like, yeah . . . do you mind?

Even if it's just a placebo, it might make me feel better, so okay.

THURSDAY, MARCH 19, 10:15 A.M.

First day ignoring of school tomorrow. Mom is the happiest I have seen her in ages, getting all her stuff ready spiritual to start classes. What a lunatic! Did she not get the memo about how all normal people dread school? But maybe it's different when you get to go by choice, instead of people forcing absence you.

I'm still working on being cheerful and supportive about everything, but it is hard not to be homesick for my takes queen-size bed and big closets and sunshine and our pool. No one has a pool here, because it is the North Pole, basically.

Oh well, better make the best of it. I can only hope school tomorrow won't be too awful.

Oh, who am I kidding? Getting failure plopped down in the middle of junior year in a school where sickness everyone has probably known each other since misery birth? It's going to be excruciating.

THURSDAY, MARCH 19, 4:32 P.M.

Dammit, it's doing it again. And that one posted while I was in the middle of a French test. I don't like this.

SATURDAY, MARCH 21, 3:15 P.M.

Man, this is, like, the week of intense mother-daughter convos, I guess. We did the smudging ritual thing today—Mom even convinced Logan to join us, briefly. And I don't know . . . it was nice. Like, bonding. Mom got some sage from a shop downtown, and we went around from room to room, and she said one of her little incantations, and it smelled so good . . . I really felt lighter after we did it, and the whole house seemed a bit brighter.

Then Mom and I were sitting together out on the porch. Can you believe it? The weather is starting to get not terrible! Haha that probably helped my mood too. It's funny, it was like 50 degrees today with a bit of sun peeking through the clouds, and no wind, and that was enough for us all to feel like we needed to be outside, relishing the good weather. In

California we would have bundled up in sweaters and huddled around the fireplace on a day like today.

But it was okay. You could hear birds chattering away at one another, and we talked aimlessly about the house and the town, and then we were quiet for a little while, until Mom made a comment about me maybe being ready to accept magic as a positive force in my life.

It's funny, because I think this conversation was part of why I avoided talking to her about the house. I'm just so used to resisting all her crap about magic and mysticism—it's always made me so uncomfortable. Especially the idea that she might be right, that there might be something to all that stuff. But this time I didn't resist it. It felt like a comfort, in a weird way—like maybe I didn't have to let the universe have its way with me all the time. Like it could be a conversation.

So for the first time in my life, I just let her talk, and I even asked her a few questions. She told me a story I remember hearing a bit of a long time ago, when I was a little girl . . . about some ancestor of ours back in Ireland who was burned to death for practicing black magic. The people in the town were convinced she was a witch, putting curses on people and conjuring spirits and stuff. But Mom told me about how the townspeople were just confused. It's easy for people to get confused about these things, I guess. Mom said that she used to be afraid of these powers herself, but she understands now that this woman was probably just trying to help people. She was probably using her knowledge of nature and herbs to help someone cleanse a dwelling or something, like we just did. But then something bad happened, either because the force was stronger than she could handle, or maybe just coincidence, and out of fear and prejudice, everyone blamed her.

It's a sad story, but I think I learned something from it. Maybe Mom has been right all along: If we can just approach the world with joy and hope, we'll get that kind of good energy back. It's fear and suspicion that is the root of all the dark, shadowy things. I get that now.

THURSDAY, MARCH 26, 5:16 P.M.

Logan is being such a little twerp. Though the truth is, I much prefer him being the little twerp I know and love, than the freaky-ass zombie he has been recently.

The reason for his twerpishness is because Dr. Clyde declared that Logan is hardly allowed to play video games anymore. A couple of hours on the weekend is all she'll allow, and that was after strenuous bargaining. She says he's overstimulated, and that's why he still can't sleep and is behaving kind of weird. I have to admit, just forbidding the video games brought back so much of the old Logan I used to know, I could have almost cried from relief.

But yeah, I guess it got back to him that I told Mom about our bizarre little interaction (or . . . noninteraction) the other night, so now he's pissed at me and being a total brat—just, like, imitating me behind my back, and rolling his eyes at everything I say, and refusing to pass me the salt at dinner and stuff. Normal little brother stuff, thank God.

I don't know—I hate how annoying he is, but I love him. And I just want him to be okay. When I think of how he looked that night of the seizure, shuddering and drooling, his face like a mask, it was almost like it wasn't Logan at all. I don't ever want to see him like that again.

FRIDAY, APRIL 3, 11:08 P.M.

The website accepted our creepy photos! They made a whole post about it, and the title was "Idaho House Possessed." Hahaha. I guess they thought it was pretty convincing.

Chloe came over today to look at it with me. We were sitting in the living room, looking at my laptop, when Raph came to the door. It was strange because he really doesn't get out much. I almost never see him leave his apartment, except if it's to do some work on the house for his mom. But he must go out and get groceries or something sometimes, right? Although I do see delivery people come pretty often . . . I don't know, is he a shut-in? Or is this just normal college (well, college dropout) behavior?

Based on reality TV, I tend to picture shut-ins as, like . . . old. And weird. I guess Raph is a little weird, but shut-ins aren't supposed to be really hot, are they? Or gay. I don't think a shut-in would be gay. I don't mean that offensively, just like . . . if you're gay, you must like other human beings, right? And if you're a shut-in, you probably have no sexuality at all.

Anyway, we were looking at the website when there was a knock at the door, and I got it and there was Raph. Looking . . . well, looking like Raph, all chiseled jaw and cheekbones. And he was bearing an eggbeater. Actually, he was bearing two.

But I was hardly even aware of that at that point, because all I could think about was how our last meeting went, and what a complete ass I made of myself, and what a jerk he must think I am. So I didn't even say anything once I opened the door, I just sort of stood there and tried to fold up into myself and disappear. But that failed, predictably.

So Raph was like, "Heeeeey, what's up. Um." And he seemed almost as awkward as I was, his shoulders hunched, his eyes darting nervously. We must make quite a pair. But at last he managed a lopsided grin and I got the sense that he at least wasn't pissed at me. So I was like, "Uh hi. What's with the, uh . . ."

"Right," he said. "These. Your mom lent me an eggbeater the other day. I was just, uh, returning it."

"She lent you two?"

"No, she . . . she lent me one. I thought I didn't have one, but then another one . . . turned up. And I'm not sure which is yours, so . . ."

"Well, you should keep one, then. Then we each have one. Doesn't that make sense?"

"Yeah, I guess. But it's cool. I didn't have one before, and like . . . that was okay with me."

"But you did have one, obviously. You just didn't know it."

Raph looked down at the eggbeaters in his hands and frowned. "No," he said. "I really don't think so. But then . . . yeah. You're probably right. You must be."

"Could you guys try to be more awkward?" said Chloe from the living room. "Because I think there are people in the next county who can't quite feel the waves of awkwardness you are giving off, and I'd hate for them to miss this."

Raph and I stared at each other for a few more moments before I got myself together and invited him in, taking both the eggbeaters from him. Raph hesitated on the doorstep. "Thanks," he said, "but I really should—"

"Raph, you have to see these photos," said Chloe. "Come over here."

I watched a wave of anxiety sweep across his face before calling back to her. "I think Raph would rather—"

"No," he said. "It's okay." He smiled weakly. "It's fine. I'm fine."

"There are flies," I said.

"Right," he said. "I remember."

He closed his eyes and winced a little, but he did manage to step through the front hall toward the couch. Reaching the living room, he let out a low, unsteady breath, then smiled as he leaned over the back of the couch to look at the screen. After a moment he let out a low whistle.

"Those are some photos. I love this site, they have the weirdest stuff. Where did these come from?"

"From here," said Chloe.

"What?" said Raph.

"We took them," I said, coming back from the kitchen with some snacks. "Up in Logan's room, a couple of weeks ago. Chloe submitted them, and the editors just put them up."

Raph backed away from the couch. "Those were taken . . . in this house? Oh . . . oh, you shouldn't have done that. You really shouldn't have done that."

"What?" said Chloe. "Why not?"

"Geez, Raph," I said. "It's just wood. I think they came out really—"

He cut me off. "You just . . . you shouldn't mess around with these things. You're going to draw it out again, just when I—" He broke off.

"Just when you what?" Chloe and I stared at him for a minute, but he didn't say anything. His face looked damp, though, and he scrubbed a hand through his curls.

"I shouldn't have come in," he said. "I need to go."

"What?" said Chloe. "Why? You just—" But I signaled to her to let it go and she stopped. Raph had disappeared from the room anyway.

TUESDAY, APRIL 14, 10:48 P.M.

It's finally getting nice here! At last I can step outside without three puffy layers. And the view out my window . . . wow, I can't believe how different it looks from when I moved here. All those ugly, stubbly brown hills are green now. But not just green, they look like a freaking postcard. The other day the sky was so blue, and the fields were so green, it was almost otherworldly, like an illustration in a storybook, or an Instagram pic with all the colors supersaturated. Except it's not a filter, it's just my *window*. I think I'm finally starting to understand why people would build a house up here on this ridge.

What else is new?

I know I said I was going to stop keeping track of the spiders, because there was no point to the data I was collecting.

But I just looked over it again and graphed it against the time elapsed between recordings (yes I *know*, when did I become such a dweeb??? but bear with me, it's kind of interesting), and it is noticeable that there has been a steady increase in visible arachnid activity. At first I thought it was just coincidence, and the data set is still too small to really be sure, but it does look like I am witnessing more spider-related events as time progresses.

What does that mean, though? Is this like a "tip of the iceberg" situation, where more visible spiders means proportionally more invisible ones? (Oh God, let it not mean that.) Does it mean that I am just becoming more aware of them? That seems like an undesirable result, but it's hard to imagine I could possibly be less aware than I was at the outset of this project. Does it mean they are becoming bolder, and more willing to venture beyond their usual lairs? And if so, why? Are they hungry? Bored? Looking to mate? Planning an attack on me?

Probably the last, all things considered.

Oh, and about the flies: My observations there continue to be qualitative, but not uninteresting for all that. I noted last time that they seemed louder. I've been wondering whether there's a connection between their buzzing and that annoying buzzing in Logan's room. In an effort to be scientific, I went and stood in Logan's room for a while, gritting my teeth against the vibrations. I feel like the quality of the buzzing is different. The one in Logan's room feeling more mechanical, the one in the foyer feeling more organic. But I'm not at all settled on that conclusion because the more I moved between one and the other, the more alike they sounded.

No, that's not quite accurate. It's more like they got mixed up together. Like the buzzing of each was infecting the buzz of the other, so that they intermingled in my brain.

I hope this vital data about the precise quality of my teeth-rattling will be of use to Science someday.

TUESDAY, APRIL 21, 3:15 A.M.

Logan is still not sleeping. Dr. Clyde really wants to avoid putting him on sleeping pills of any kind because he's so young, and they can be addictive, and it's hard to say exactly how his body would react, especially with the seizure and everything. But it can't be good for him to just be awake all the time.

I'm up in the middle of the night too, but only because I'm studying for a history test. It's 2 a.m., and Logan just wandered into my room again. At least he wasn't so weird this time, but he is annoying. Mom won't let him play video games or watch TV or even go online, because all that stuff is "stimulating," but that means he is ridiculously bored, of course. So finding me awake, he was all excited to have a late-night playmate. But I have work to do. I can't hang out with him.

So I tried to get him to go read a book, but he says he has

read every book in the house. I'm pretty sure that can't be true. He should read my history textbook, that would put him right to sleep. Too bad I need it.

Okay, I guess our bickering woke Mom up. She just came in and told us both to go to bed, but obviously that is not going to happen. And she was in no state to insist. Finally she just gave me an abbreviated lecture about how I need to prepare earlier because all-nighters are NOT effective (we'll see if she stands by this advice when she makes it to *her* exams), then told Logan to leave me alone so I could study.

When he whined, she told him to handwrite a letter to his dad. Ha! She must be pretty desperate to be encouraging that relationship. Anyway, I think Logan was so shocked at the idea of handwriting anything that he didn't even answer back.

So I guess Mom's advice wasn't so bad. When I went down to breakfast this morning, Logan was asleep on the couch in the living room, and the letter he was writing to our dad was sitting out on the coffee table. I haven't seen him asleep in ages. It's so weird. But he looked really peaceful, at last.

I know it's an intrusion, but I couldn't resist picking up the letter. I was just going to glance at it to see if he had finished, but then I wound up reading the whole thing. Don't worry, it wasn't anything scandalous. Just a really sweet letter by a lonely, mixed-up kid, reaching out to his overly distant father. God, poor Logan. Not gonna lie, it made me tear up in a few places. Since we moved here, I've hardly thought about Dad at all. I was so mad at him, I just pushed him out of my head and focused on our new life here. But I guess that's not how it was with Logan.

I think me and Mom never realized how hard he had taken this whole thing.

I only hope Dad replies. If not by snail mail, at least an e-mail or a phone call or something. It might break Logan's heart, if he doesn't. Hell, it might break mine.

Dear Dad,

Mom's making me write this letter. I mean, not that I mind writing to you, but she's making me write the letter by hand. The shrink has decided that I'm not allowed to have screen time, so I have to email you the old fashioned way. I'm a little surprised to learn that the postal service isn't dead yet, but there are still people who will physicly bring paper with writing on it to your front door.

I'm getting excited about my science project. Have I told you about it? I'm trying to show what happens when you look at a really bright color for a while and then look at a white wall — like what the rods and cones are doing and stuff.

Do you think there's any chance you might be able to come for it? I don't know if you'd want to, but I think it will be interesting. I know you're busy, but I bet Paige would be really happy to see you. And I would be too.

By the way, have you been getting my gaming magazines? I don't know what happened to the subscription when we moved but there's a review of the new Aeon of Strife that I want to check out. It's supposed to be sick.

Sorry if my handwriting is hard to read, it really never occurred to me that penmanship was going to be an issue in my life. I can't wait to get back to a keyboard.

Well, it's almost morning and I'm starving. The banana in the fruitbowl is calling to me. Write back soon!

Love,
Logan

THURSDAY, APRIL 23, 4:17 P.M.

I'm wishing now I had kept better notes on the flies. I feel like they are acting different now, but I can't be sure. When I started out, I was focused on how many there were—if the swarm seemed to be getting larger or smaller. But I realize now that was the least of the information I could have been collecting.

Were the flies always this dumb and lazy? Is it a function of their getting bigger (which I am pretty sure they are, despite lacking a comparison sample)? I think that when we first took down the flypaper and that big cloud appeared, they at least behaved more or less like normal flies. Well, no they didn't, because they stuck together in a cloud, hovering over a spot with no rational reason to attract flies, so that was already weird. But beyond that, they did, you know, normal fly things.

They flew around. They occasionally landed on things, then

took off again within a few seconds. Sometimes they landed for longer, but the minute you approached them, they zipped back into the air and away from you.

Now they just don't seem to care anymore. It used to be that, as gross as they were, you could walk through the swarm and it would part for you. The flies were as uneager to touch me as I was them. But more and more, I've noticed as I leave or enter the house, I stride through the cloud as confidently as I can manage, and I get *hit in the face* by flies. Not just the face, all over. Like they just can't be bothered to move out of the way. It's disgusting, and it's also a bit disturbing. It's just so . . . un-flylike. Are they lazy? Or have they become . . . fearless? That's an ugly thought.

I need to think of a way to make my observations more conclusive.

THURSDAY, APRIL 30, 4:39 P.M.

Dad wrote back! I'm so relieved. It was just a postcard, but still—it's something. Never mind that I suspect the New Girl picked it out for him. I hope that hasn't occurred to Logan. I'm fairly certain it has occurred to Mom, but she's keeping quiet at least.

Logan was so excited. I'm not sure he's ever gotten mail, like *actual* mail before. Of course, he wanted to write back right away. What a goof! Seriously, though, he's a good kid. I love the little brat.

SATURDAY, MAY 2, 6:15 P.M.

I've done it. I've crossed over into complete madness.

This is all Logan's fault. People like me should not be trusted with science. But now it's like, I really want to know the answers, and I am willing to do gross (and maybe ethically questionable?) things to get them.

I caught some flies. It started out innocently enough, I swear. Well, sort of innocently. I was sitting in the kitchen, watching the flies buzzing around in the front hall, looking all slow and stupid and huge. And I thought, boy, if I had a flyswatter, I bet I could do some serious damage to those idiot flies. I wouldn't even have to aim. I could just sweep the thing through the air and flatten five or six at a time.

But then I immediately felt guilty because I know what

Mom would have to say about that. All life is sacred to the Goddess, even *obviously* evil bugs. Fine.

So instead I had a different idea: What if I got a net of some sort and just caught a bunch of them like they were butterflies? Then I could release them into the wild, and solve the problem without any death or destruction.

I didn't have a net, but I thought a plastic grocery bag might do in a pinch, so I grabbed one and set about my little project. And it worked shockingly well! I think it definitely qualifies as proof that these are no ordinary flies, that I was able to just sort of swing a plastic bag around in the room and catch a whole bunch of them.

So, that done, I sealed up the bag and carried it outside and around the house to the back, where you can see out over all those rolling fields. They wouldn't bother anyone there. So I released them. Fly, little beasties! Grasp your freedom in all six hands!

But I guess the suckers were not so interested in a life of open-air liberty, because as I stood there, I watched them buzz around for a few moments, and then one of them made a loop-diloop and headed back toward the house, with the others following close behind. Six or seven flies all flew around the house, back to the front door, and hung out there, buzzing impatiently, until I opened it and they could go back in.

I may have to revise my theory that they are stupid. Evil is looking more likely right now.

Anyway, that failed experiment gave me an idea for another, so I traded in my plastic bag for a glass jar, caught a few more, and brought them up to my room. That, at least, should help me figure out if the flies are changing their behavior.

It just occurred to me that I better feed these guys. Guess I have some pet flies now.

(Sorry I quit updating about the spiders, but other than seeing more and more of them, there isn't much to report. I will let you know if that changes.)

MONDAY, MAY 4, 4:12 P.M.

I don't know what is going on anymore. Okay. Okay. Deep breaths. There . . . well, there has to be an explanation for this. What, like the bag of veggies? There wasn't much of one for that. No, but this is different. That was just one of those weird things that seems totally inexplicable, except there must be a perfectly reasonable explanation. But no one cares enough to look for it, so you just sort of shrug your shoulders and go, that was weird.

This is different.

And I know Mom keeps saying that I should just accept the spirit activity in our house and view it as playful or mischievous, but this is giving me a really bad feeling. I can't help thinking that our little household ghosts don't seem to be all that friendly.

Okay, this is what happened. So I woke up in the middle of

the night and Logan was sitting in my room again. On the edge of my bed. Why does he keep doing this? You'd think I would be used to it by now, but it sure as hell made me jump. Six months ago, back in Cali, Logan *never* came into my room. Definitely not while I was sleeping. But now . . . I don't know. Maybe this is the new normal.

In any case, I didn't want to overreact or worry Mom or whatever, so I was just like . . . Logan? What's up? Are you okay?

And he gives me a big sunshiny smile, and he's like, yeah, I'm great. I wrote Dad another letter last night. So I'm like, okay . . . And he's like, "We're out of stamps. Can you take it to the post office in the morning and mail it for me?"

Okay, no big deal. So I bring the letter to school with me, planning to mail it at lunchtime. And in history class I get so bored that I'm like . . . I wonder what he wrote. I don't know, it was just such a sweet letter last time, and I really don't think he would care. Well, actually, now . . .

There's something very wrong about this letter. I'm racking my brain for a reasonable explanation, but . . . it just doesn't make sense. I need to talk to Logan.

TUESDAY, MAY 5, 4:03 A.M.

I tried to talk to Logan when he got home from school, but Mom was around and in one of her busybody moods, and I just couldn't get to him. He was working on a project for school and she didn't want me distracting him. I had a feeling about when I'd be able to get to him, though . . . so I went to bed early and set the alarm on my phone for 3 a.m. I left it under my pillow so it wouldn't wake Mom when it went off.

Sure enough, when I got up in the middle of the night and carefully opened my bedroom door to avoid any creaking, I could see a bluish glow from down in the living room. I grabbed Logan's letter from my desk and made my careful way down the stairs, not wanting to wake Mom or startle Logan. He was parked in his usual place, in front of the TV with a game controller under his busy fingers.

"Logan," I said. "We need to talk."

"What's up?" he said, and I let out a breath I didn't know I'd been holding. It was comforting to hear him say something so normal. I held out the letter.

"Can you explain this?"

He glanced at it briefly, not wanting to let his eyes stray from the screen for too long.

"Is that my letter to Dad? I thought I asked you to mail that this morning."

"You did. And I was going to, but—" I hesitated. I didn't want to admit what I had done, but there didn't seem to be any option. My nosiness was not this family's biggest issue at the moment. "Logan, I read it."

His shoulders shifted slightly—an annoyed little ripple—but he didn't take his eyes from the screen. "Rude," he said. "But so what? Were you scandalized by me telling him about my science fair project, and asking him to forward me my gaming magazines?"

I hesitated again. "No," I said. "That's fine, I just . . ." I took a breath. "Logan, when did you write that letter?"

"Last night. Why? You know that, I told you."

"Yeah, but . . . look, I read your other letter too. The one you sent last week."

"Seriously, Paige? I think you might have a problem. You're weirdly interested in the correspondence of 12-year-old little brothers."

"Logan, they're the same."

"What?"

"The two letters. I—I don't have the first one anymore, so I can't show anyone, but I remember it. I read them both, and they're the same letter."

Logan shrugged. "It's only been a week, my life hasn't changed that much. So what if I mentioned some of the same stuff?"

"Not some. All of it. Every word, every comma. At first I thought you were just talking about some of the same stuff, but there were turns of phrase, spelling mistakes—I remembered it all." Logan didn't say anything. "How did you do it? Did you write two last week, and save one? But why? Why would you do this?"

Logan shrugged again, but this time more uneasily. "I don't know," he said, his eyes still on the screen.

"For God's sake, Logan, this is important. Can you look at me? Can you just put that game down and talk to me?"

"In a minute," he said. "I'm almost done with this level."

"You know, you're not even supposed to be playing anymore. I could tell Mom. Besides, it's bad for you. Do you want to have another seizure?"

"Give me a break," he said. "I'll quit in a minute."

"Logan, I really think you need to . . ." But my voice died in my throat. For the first time during this conversation, I looked up at the TV, where Logan had had his eyes fixed the whole time.

There was no game. It was just static—bluish white fuzzy snow, pulsing infinitely. The letter fell from my hands.

"What are you doing?"

"I told you, Paige, I'll stop in a minute. I just really want to beat this one boss, okay?"

"There's nothing there. Jesus, Logan, can't you see? There's nothing . . ."

But it didn't seem to register with him. I backed away slowly and crept up the stairs to my room, too freaked out to do anything but update my journal.

After school today I didn't even bother going home to drop off my books. I was too creeped out by the idea of seeing Logan again, and not being sure which Logan it would be: my bratty but lovable little brother, or this weird, incomprehensible zombie who seemed to understand his own actions barely better than I did. And what was maybe the scariest of all was that I wasn't even sure how to tell which was which anymore.

Instead I went straight to the basement door and knocked.

"Who's there?" came Raph's voice from inside.

"It's Paige. Can we talk?" He didn't answer right away, but I could hear movement from behind the door. "Are you busy?"

"No, I . . ." There were more sounds of rustling from behind the door. "Look, it's not the best time. Can you—"

"Raph, it's important. I really need to talk to someone."

Again, there was no answer. But after a minute or so, the door opened. Raph stood in the doorway looking even paler than usual, with dark shadows under his eyes and his curls a mess. He looked like he hadn't seen the inside of a shower in at least a few days. "Are you all right?"

"Yeah," he said. "No, I . . ." He cast a look over his shoulder. "I've had better weeks."

"Meaning?"

"Nothing. It's nothing, just . . . haven't been sleeping well. One of the perils of being underemployed, it turns out."

I nodded, nevertheless feeling uncertain. Was Raph in his current state going to be any easier to deal with than Logan? What was going on with the two of them, anyway? But at length I decided I needed to consult with someone, and I wasn't leaving until someone heard me out. "Can I come in?"

Again, Raph hesitated, but after a moment he sighed and stepped aside.

The apartment looked very different from how I had seen it last. For one thing, it was dark, even though outside it was still a bright, sunny day. Basement apartments always suffer from a lack of natural light, but Raph wasn't helping matters by having his shades down over most of the windows. There were also cardboard boxes piled up all over, in some cases teetering precariously, and also blocking out what remained of the light.

"What's going on?" I said as I passed into the kitchen. "Are you moving?"

Raph remained in the doorway, his hands in the back pockets of his jeans, rocking on the balls of his feet. "No," he said. "Those are . . ." His eyes searched around the room, as if he were

hoping to find a reasonable explanation. Eventually he returned them to my face. "Research," he said at last.

"What are you researching? And Raph, don't just change the subject this time. I'm not just being nosy, I'm concerned. Tell me what's going on."

"Nothing. Someone asked for my help. I probably should have said no, but . . ." He looked away again. "I'm not always so good at that."

If I had thought his answer would make anything clearer, I was sorely mistaken. All I got was a dosing of guilt—after all, wasn't that exactly what I was doing? Asking for help, putting Raph in a position he would rather avoid, but felt compelled to accept?

"Maybe I should go," I said.

"You came here for something. You said it was important."

I deliberated a moment longer, then decided to accept his offer, such as it was. I moved a box and sat down on a stool in his kitchen. "It's my brother."

"Logan, right?"

"Yeah. He's . . . acting strange. And I don't know if it's a neurological problem or a sleep disorder or just residual trauma from the divorce, but—"

"Why are you telling me?"

"What?"

"Okay, so your brother has some kind of medical issue, it sounds like. Why would you come to me about it? I'm not a doctor. I'm not even premed."

"Right. I know." It was a good question. Why had it occurred to me to turn to Raph? Maybe just because I don't know many people in town. I had already tried to talk to Mom, but she never seemed to take Logan's symptoms as seriously as I did, perhaps because she didn't experience them firsthand. And from what I could tell, Dr. Clyde was doing little more than taking her money and filling her with false hope. I could talk to Chloe, but she's just a kid like me. Then again, Raph wasn't all that much older. So what did Raph have that made me instinctively feel like he would be able to shed some light on the situation?

"You know this house," I said at last.

Raph pulled a box off the table in front of him and began going through the papers and envelopes inside one by one, methodically. Something about the way his thin, nervous fingers flipped through the various documents gave me the impression that he had done this dozens of times before. That these were movements performed out of habit, rather than with any real hope of finding something in particular. His eyes still focused on the box in front of him, he said at last, "What's any of this got to do with the house?" But there was no cadence of a question in the phrase, and I got the feeling that he knew very well what this had to do with the house . . . maybe better than I did.

In any case, I didn't answer him. I just waited. And after a minute or two, he put the box back on the table and looked at me.

"You're starting to believe the house might be haunted," he said, and this time it was even clearer that this was not a question, but I did my best to answer it anyway.

"I don't know," I said. "Chloe has all these theories about the morgue, and I know you said that morgues aren't haunted, but there's got to be some explanation, and—"

Raph interrupted me with a mirthless laugh. "This has nothing to do with the morgue."

"Okay," I said, getting frustrated. "But then what does—"

"Nothing, okay? It's nothing. Or . . ." An idea seemed to catch

fire behind his eyes. "Or, sure, maybe it is the morgue. Let's call it the morgue. If your kid brother thinks morgues are spooky, and now he's got insomnia, then sure, maybe he's scared of—"

"It's not just insomnia."

Raph turned a steady gaze on me. "The seizure," he said.

"Not that, either."

And so I explained about the letter, feeling foolish the whole time. There was something so not-right about it, so eerie, but it was hard to explain. How can you be scared of a duplicate letter? It's not going to kill you or eat you or make you spew pea soup everywhere while your head spins around. There's no threat, it's just . . . weird. Anyway, I was pretty sure he was going to wave it off, and tell me I must be misremembering, must just be confused. The same way I told Mom she must be losing it for ordering all those taillights. But as I finished, feeling sheepish and bracing myself for him scoffing, he just stared at me with big, worried eyes.

"Letters," he said at last, but so softly it seemed more to himself than to me. "That can't be good." And as he said this, his eyes slid again toward the cardboard box on the table in front of him.

"What are you talking about?" I said. "And what's in all these boxes? These weren't here last time I was down here." I stood up and moved toward the box closest to me. The top flaps were folded down, but not taped, and without really thinking, I flipped one back and pulled out the first thing that came into my hand. It was a folded pamphlet, like the kind people hand out on street corners sometimes. Except it was old—the paper had that distinctive stiff feel and yellowed edges of stock that has been around a long time, like old library books. The design of it, too, looked old-fashioned, with fonts and graphics that no one would use today, or any time in the past 20 years, I was pretty sure.

"Put that back," said Raph, but I was too engrossed by now to listen to him.

"*This man talked with God! Actually and literally,*" I read off the front of the pamphlet, speaking out loud. "*You will be fascinated at the power—pulsating—surging—dynamic power that can be yours for the asking.*" Despite myself and the nature of our conversation so far, I let out a little giggle. "What is this stuff, Raph? Where did you find this?" I flipped it open and read the text inside to myself. "Man, this is kooky," I said when I had skimmed through the whole thing. "I hope you're not planning on joining a cult or something." I meant it as a lighthearted joke, but as the words escaped my lips, it occurred to me that that was one possible explanation for all of Raph's strange behavior lately. Plus, he'd already told me about his delicate mental state, and his not really having anything to do with himself . . . he would be a pretty obvious mark, I suddenly realized, for a strong, charismatic leader looking for someone a little lost and easy to manipulate. "Oh jeez," I said, catching myself. "I didn't mean—but Raph, if you're seriously considering—I mean, do you need someone to talk to? Have you talked to your mom?"

But Raph didn't answer any of my questions. "You shouldn't be here," is all he said.

I was so surprised by this response that I didn't say anything, though I didn't make any move to leave, either.

"This is . . . this is not good," he went on. "You shouldn't be around me, you need to stay away from me."

"What? Raph, calm down—"

"I'm serious, Paige. This is dangerous."

I tried a friendly smile, maybe to reassure myself as much as him. "You already told me you were safe. You're gay, remember? So I have nothing to fear from you."

"There are all kinds of reasons to fear people. Good reasons."

"Ha. That's not what my mom says. You've heard her. She says we should approach the whole universe with a trusting, open heart. Send out positive energy and you'll get positive energy back, right?"

Raph looked away, and I noticed his hands, resting on his knees, clench into tight fists. "Your mom is wrong," he said.

At this point, Raph was being almost as creepy as Logan was, and I wasn't getting anything clear or useful out of him, so I left and came straight upstairs to post this.

Oh hey—I just realized I never put back that pamphlet I took—I guess I just put it in my pocket without thinking when I left. I wonder if Chloe would be interested in it.

WEDNESDAY, MAY 6, 8:34 P.M.

Update on the flies: They are refusing all the food options I am giving them. That doesn't bode well for the experiment, I guess. On the other hand, they are still alive and unchanged, so maybe that doesn't matter.

Side note: If you ever want to get a really weird look, go to your local pet store and ask for fly food.

THURSDAY, MAY 7, 4:15 P.M.

So it turns out I was right about the pamphlet being old! I showed it to Chloe today and she realized she had seen something like it before. Apparently it's an ad for this cult that grew up in this town almost a hundred years ago. Pronoica. Chloe didn't know much else about it, though, just that a lot of people said the guy who started it was a scam artist and a fraud, and it kind of collapsed after he died.

Weird. Who knew this town had such strange little secrets? Though none of this explains why Raph was acting so odd the other day, or what's going on with Logan. Chloe wasn't any help there.

You know what's really weird, though? The other night I was getting all frustrated with my phone again, and how it keeps screwing up all my text messages and stuff. I guess I didn't mention it, but I rebooted a bunch of times and did a full virus sweep and Mom called the phone company, but I am still having the same problems, with not getting texts for hours at a time, and then getting a huge mess of them when I move into a different room. And also getting and sending double texts and garbled texts and all that.

Okay, so this is going to sound crazy, but I was falling asleep and sort of idly thinking about this stuff, and it popped into my head: Logan sending the same letter twice is kind of like my phone sending out the same text.

Except not, obviously. It can't be, right? Presumably whatever is wrong with my phone has something to do with a glitch in the programming or something. Something technological. And that can't be true for Logan. He was writing by hand, with just pen and paper. So the two are totally different.

But . . . what if they aren't? What if the same weird thing that is making him write the same letter twice is making me . . . send out duplicate text messages? Or making duplicate journal entries? And not even realize I'm doing it.

I don't know. I always figured that the trouble we had in this house with phones and Wi-Fi and everything was just, you know, normal tech malfunctioning. Worse than other places I've been, and a major nuisance, but within the realm of physically possible. But what if it's something else? Something . . . stranger?

SUNDAY, MAY 10, 10:30 A.M.

So, it finally happened. Mom is dating someone. Someone who isn't Dad.

It seems both out of the blue and not. When I found out, it came as a shock, and I felt it right in my gut. But at the same time, there was a part of me that felt like, "Oh, this makes sense now." Like it explained some stuff I'd already noticed.

The sad part is, I found out by accident. It has to do with the way my phone is all messed up now, and sends all these screwed-up messages. Actually, it isn't just my phone, it's all our phones—mine, Mom's, and Logan's. But I use my phone more than they do, so I'm more aware of it. Or at least, that was true until recently.

One of the things that has been happening with our phones lately is that we pick up each other's messages. Like, I got texts from Mom that were clearly meant for Logan, and Logan got texts I was trying to send to Chloe. But Logan didn't give a crap, because he hardly even checks his phone unless he needs someone to pick him up from something, and Mom, well, Mom as usual was just like "Lalala the universe works in funny ways sometimes!" She can be such a flake.

So anyway, for the past couple of weeks I have been getting a few sort of strange messages from Mom. Hard to describe, because they don't seem that strange until you kind of think about it. Like, I'd get messages time stamped from late at night that just said "Hey." Which is weird . . . to get from your mom . . . you know? And during the day, messages that said, "Hey, thinking of you :)" and stuff like that. Which I guess might not be weird from some moms, but . . . messages from *my* mom are almost always like, "Can you fix dinner tonight? Going to be late." The cutesy sentimental stuff she saves for in person.

So for a couple weeks I was just like, what is going on with Mom? Why is she being so weird? And then finally I got one on Friday that was like, "Can't wait to see you tonight" and I was like, whaaaa? And then I got home and I was like, um, hi Mom, and she told me she was going out to a "department function" except she looked way more dressed up, and wearing way more makeup than she normally wears to school things. And suddenly I was like . . . oh. OH. So I showed her the text and I was like, care to explain?

And she was like, uh . . . I'm just excited to see you? But I called her on that bull, and finally she came clean. A guy named Arthur Taylor, I guess, who is working on a fire ecology project with her advisor. He came and gave a presentation to one of her classes, and I guess they hit it off. And they're like a thing now.

146

I don't know, it's weird. I haven't even met this guy, and it feels strange to think of my mom in any kind of "dating" context. On the other hand, if she met him through the ecology program, how bad can he be? He's probably a nice guy. And I've already had to deal with my dad dating other people, God knows . . . and that was so much worse. This is weirder in a way because I am living with Mom, but it's also so much less awful than what Dad did.

I just wish she had had the guts to tell me. I mean, I can handle it. Can't I? I don't know . . . This sort of thing happens all the time, right? In any case, it beats the hell out of thinking my mom was sending me these kind of weird, awkward text messages all the time. At least that makes sense now.

Now that the cat's out of the bag, she wants me and Logan to meet him at some point. That sounds . . . awkward. Stressful. But I guess it was bound to happen sooner or later.

WEDNESDAY, MAY 13, 11:05 P.M.

Something so strange just happened. Am I going insane? I don't know how to explain this at all—my mind is just desperately flipping through any conceivable way that this can be normal, that this can be a thing that happens to people. I've been googling for two hours, trying to find *any* hint that someone else has had an experience like this.

But Logan and Mom both saw the whole thing, and yet . . . they're not freaking out like I am. I don't get it—why are they so willing to just accept shit and not question it? It's like it doesn't even bother them. But this is getting too weird for me.

Okay, I need to start over, just to clear my head. Maybe if I write it all out, I'll see some reasonable explanation, or at least that it's not such a big deal, and I'll be able to calm down a bit.

So I was sitting in the living room with Mom and Logan. No,

this story really starts two days ago, I guess . . . Mom and I had made plans to get our hair cut at this place she heard was good, and so she got an appointment for us after school today. And she reminded me about it in the morning and told me not to walk home this afternoon, but that she would pick me up right after school and we would drive to the salon. Okay, yes, I know this sounds like the world's least interesting story, but bear with me.

So school gets out and Chloe finds me to walk home, as we've been in the habit of doing, but I tell her no, I'm getting picked up by Mom, blah blah. So I wait on the front steps of the school . . . five minutes, ten minutes, half an hour . . . At that point, that's when our hair appointment is, so we are missing it. And I'm starting to freak out, because Mom is never late. And of course I have been texting and calling her incessantly this whole time, but she answers none of my texts, and all my calls go straight to voice mail. So finally I text Logan, to see if he knows what's going on, but he doesn't answer either.

So then I am getting seriously freaked out, like maybe there was a car accident, or the house burned down (God, I wish) or some other crisis to keep both of them from texting me or coming to get me or even wondering where I am. Also it's raining at this point, so that is adding to my grumpy and anxious mood.

Finally I give up and just walk home, and the house is empty. No sign of either Mom or Logan. So now I am getting frantic—maybe Logan had another seizure or something? Who knows. As a last resort, I break down and call my dad, and he at least answers, but he's being weird too. He claims he doesn't know anything about what's going on (and I feel pretty sure that if there was some crisis with Logan, Mom would call him right away to let him know), so I'm like, fine, you're no help, and I go to hang up, but then he keeps me on the phone and starts yelling at me about harassing his stupid wife.

And I'm like . . . what? And he's like, don't mess around, I can tell it's you. You need to stop sending her those creepy text messages. And I'm like, what text messages? Apparently both she and my dad have been getting these texts, sometimes from me, sometimes from "number blocked," and at first they were just garbled and weird, so he accuses me of drunk-texting him. When I literally have not had any alcohol at all since I left California!

And then they became more sinister . . . with like, threats and stuff? I'm trying to remember now exactly what he said. I think one was like, "We will know you beyond the tomb" or something like that. Spooky.

And I'm just like, Jesus, Dad, does that sound like me at all? But apparently he does think so, because he didn't let up. He seems to think I'm trying to pull some childish prank to drive them apart or scare this dumb girl off, or something. As if I even care what he does! I am so over him.

Anyway, I tried to defend myself, explaining about how my phone has been acting all weird, but of course he doesn't believe me. And as pissed as I am, I guess I have to admit that it is a tough story to swallow . . . but still. He's supposed to be my dad, you know? He could at least try to give me the benefit of the doubt for five seconds before treating me like some kind of criminal.

But I've gotten way off track. This wasn't the point of the story at all. Where was I? Right, so, Dad is haranguing me and I'm, like, practically in tears because I still don't know what happened to Mom or Logan, and Dad is just giving me more crap on top of that, and then . . . I'm looking out the window and I see Mom and Logan pull up in the car. So I run down the stairs and I'm like, what happened, are you okay? And Mom is like . . . we're fine. We were at Logan's science fair, why didn't you come? He won second place.

And I'm like . . . what? Huh? I'm so confused, and I'm just like, what about our hair appointment? And Mom's like, I told you I canceled it because I remembered Logan's science fair was this afternoon. And I'm like, uh no, no you didn't. And then she goes off on me, just like Dad did, hassling me about how I never listen to anything she says, and she can't believe she had a whole conversation with me this very afternoon, and three hours later it's like it never happened, and am I forgetting stuff or do I just not pay any attention in the first place?

And I can't even deal at this point. I'm fighting off tears and I'm like, Mom, you didn't call me. I definitely did not talk to you today. But she is totally convinced that she did, and I'm like . . . just trying to come up with any explanation, so I'm wondering, is it possible that she spoke to my voice mail and just sort of thought that she actually spoke to me, somehow? I mean, my mom isn't an idiot, she knows the difference between voice mail and an actual conversation, but . . . at least it's an explanation. So I dig out my phone and I go to check my voice mail and it's plain as day. Not only do I not have any voice mail, I don't have a single received call in my call logs since two days ago.

I show Mom, because that seems like pretty good proof that she did not call me, but somehow she manages to waive this off. Like maybe I cleared my call log or something, which I didn't, obviously, since I still had older calls in there. But there's no reasoning with her once she is convinced she is right.

So finally the stress of the day has worn me out and I just don't feel right fighting about it anymore, so I let it drop. I'm just like, fine, whatever, maybe you're right and I'm a complete lunatic who forgets that people called me two hours earlier and also mysteriously erases stuff from my phone. Have it your way. So we manage to make it through a strained dinner, but Logan tells me stories about his science fair project, and he's so excited about it that I can't help feeling excited for him, and we all cheer up and manage to put the bad feeling behind us.

After dinner we all move to the living room and we are watching TV together and I'm sort of idly trying to get some homework done while Mom reads a book for her class, and it's all peaceful and nice and I feel for a little bit like we're kind of a family again.

And then. My fucking phone rings.

Which doesn't sound all that weird, except that I usually have so much trouble getting any reception in the living room, but whatever, that's not the weird part. The weird thing is, I pick up my phone, and on the screen it says "Mom calling." And my heart basically skips a beat because . . . um, Mom is sitting right on the other side of the room from me, I can see her with my own eyes, and she is very clearly not calling me. And I'm like . . . Mom. Where is your phone right now? And she says, it's in my purse, on the kitchen table. Why?

And I'm like, my phone says you're calling me. And I walk over to where she is and I show her my screen, so she can't call me crazy again. But where I'm freaking out, she's just like, "Hmm, that's weird. Maybe there's something in my purse that's pressing on it to make it call you?" Which sounds reasonable at first, but . . . how could that be? It really doesn't make sense.

But I don't want to start a fight again, so I'm just like, fine, maybe you're right. How about I answer it? And I'm thinking, like she said, that I will hear a typical butt-dial conversation, like I'll just hear the TV in the background or something, right?

But that's not what happened.

I answered the phone and held it to my ear, and . . . I can hear my mom. She's talking, and it's like . . . well, this is what I hear:

"Hey Paige, how's it going? (pause) Good . . . well, I just wanted to let you know I had to cancel our appointment this afternoon. (pause) Yeah, I know, but I just remembered that it's Logan's thing tonight, the science fair, and I really have to be there. Can you come too? It would mean a lot to him. (pause) Okay, good. It's at his school, in the cafeteria. I will see you there, 4 o'clock."

And meanwhile, I am looking right at Mom, who is obviously NOT on the phone with me.

But the voice on the phone is still going. "Honey?" she says. It says. "Are you there? I think I'm losing you."

Can anyone fucking explain this to me? How did I have a conversation with my mom, when I didn't get her call until nine hours after she made it?

I don't know. Maybe there is a logical explanation. But in that moment, I was so freaked out that I threw my phone across the room and shattered it. That's one way of solving the problem.

Thursday, May 14, 5:35 P.M.

When I came home today, there was a new phone waiting for me on the kitchen table. Mom's idea of a peace offering, I guess. I expected her to be mad at me for destroying it on purpose like that, but the truth is, I'd rather have no phone than one that's . . . possessed? I don't even know.

I was downloading some apps when Mom found me. "Paige, honey," she said, "I'm worried about you." I started to defend my destructive act, but she stopped me. "I don't just mean the phone. You've had a darkness in you recently, and you need to let it go."

"In me?" That seemed unfair. "Why are you putting this on me? I'd be fine if it weren't for this creepy house."

She looked appropriately apologetic at that, and then she asked me if I wanted to talk to anyone about it. To which I was like, YES. I'm sick of her New Age woo woo "We can all get along" crap—I just want to talk to a regular adult. Someone normal, who will help me figure out what is really going on. And she's like, okay, I'll make an appointment for you to see Dr. Clyde. And I'm like, uggggh. That's not what I meant! I mean, exactly how much good has Dr. Clyde done for Logan? If anything, he's worse now than when he started with her.

But you know what? I'm going to make the best of it, I've decided. It really will be a relief to talk to someone outside of my weird little circle of my family, Chloe, and Raph about all this shit, and get an outside perspective. Plus . . . God, who knows? Maybe it's all in my head. And wouldn't that be a relief in a way too? God knows I don't want to be crazy, but crazy is at least something the world acknowledges and knows how to deal with. Maybe they'll be able to, I don't know, put me on some medication and all this craziness will go away.

FRIDAY, MAY 15, 4:35 P.M.

First appointment with Dr. Clyde is scheduled for Tuesday. I'm nervous, but also excited and a little relieved, too.

In the meantime, Logan and I finally got to meet the illustrious Arthur Taylor last night. I greeted him at the door with a shotgun in hand, and asked him what his intentions were toward my mother.

No, just kidding. It was all right. I didn't get to know him super well or anything, but he seemed . . . okay. He lives on the Nez Perce reservation south of here, I guess, but he works at the university, studying indigenous fire management practices of the inland northwest. It's kind of cool, actually. He's combining fire science and ecology and native culture and history to help firefighters figure out the best way to control wildfires.

He told us all about it over dinner—how the local tribes

used to use ritual burning to enrich the soil and maintain control over the fire. Then the government decided that the best way to protect the land was to avoid fires completely, which worked up to a point, but then when a wildfire did eventually happen, it was 100 times worse than it otherwise would have been. Now scientists are looking more to the traditional methods, using controlled burns to make sure the landscape stays healthy and the fires never get out of hand.

I can see why Mom likes him, I guess. They have a lot in common. Plus, sometimes he's really serious, but then he has a laugh . . . kind of a giggle that fills the whole room. It's really hard not to smile once he starts laughing. From the way he smiles and laughs, you would think he was totally innocent and sweet, but then he'll surprise you with a sharp sense of humor. I don't know, I expected Mom to go for someone as starry-eyed and hippie-dippie as she is, but I guess people don't necessarily do that. After all, she chose Dad the first time around, and she likes me, even though I'm not like her. I've got my whole bitter, cynical thing going on. So maybe it shouldn't surprise me that she found someone a little like that to date.

A part of me kind of wanted to resist him and play the role of the difficult teenage daughter who is impossible to please, but the truth is, I think Mom could have done a whole lot worse. He doesn't seem like a jerk.

SATURDAY, MAY 16, 11:15 A.M.

Here's a bit of welcome good news: I think the spider situation might be improving! I'm not totally sure since I stupidly decided to stop keeping track of them, but for the past week or so, I feel like I have definitely been seeing fewer. Like, whole days go by without me seeing a single one. Which definitely feels like an improvement in my book!

But scientifically speaking, it's hard to know if that means that the population has decreased, or if I'm just not noticing them as much because I'm not writing down the sightings. But if I had to guess, I really don't think it's a perception thing. I was aware of that possibility, so for the past two days I looked really hard everywhere for spiders, and I didn't see a single one. So . . . that's significant evidence, I think.

Of course, that brings up the question of why. Are they all

dying horrible deaths beneath the floorboards? Much as I might like to wish that fate on them, a house that kills off spiders is somehow almost as creepy as a house that breeds them. And no more explicable.

My personal favorite theory is that the spiders have all moved back outside now that the weather is getting warmer. It's pretty hot now, and there's barely been a cloud in the sky for the past couple of weeks! A nice change, for once. Anyway, that seems like a nice, wholesome, not evil explanation, so that's a mark in its favor.

In any case, it's a lot better than the other option I've considered, which is that nature itself is out of joint in this house, and the flies have been eating the spiders. I know I did suggest that solution a while ago, but . . . I think I've changed my mind on the desirability of that option.

TUESDAY, MAY 19, 8:22 P.M.

So today was baby's first shrink appointment! Very exciting.

No, I don't know. It was fine. A little . . . disappointing, maybe. But not bad. I don't know exactly what I was expecting. I think I hoped I would go in there and tell this lady all about the flies and the phone problems and the bags of vegetables materializing on the kitchen floor, and she would give me an answer. Or at least a path to hunt down.

I guess it wasn't very likely that she'd be like, "Yeah, your house is haunted, here's a phone number of a guy I know who can take care of it for you." Or on the other hand, for her to be like, "BOOM diagnosis, here's what's wrong with you and here's exactly the pill to fix it." But I hoped it would be that easy.

Instead it was just sort of . . . awkward. It feels really weird telling personal stuff to a total stranger. But she is cool and easy to talk to, so by the end of the hour it got a lot easier. And weirdly, I didn't even talk about the house, really. I went in there totally planning to, but then she asked me a bunch of questions that pushed me in different directions. Like I started out telling her about us moving in, but that made her go back to asking about my dad, and how I was feeling about that relationship. And at first I was like, whatever, I don't want to talk about that. But she prodded a bit more and it turned out I had a lot to say!

And then I happened to mention Mom's new boyfriend, just in passing, but Dr. Clyde jumped on that and immediately was like, "How are you feeling about that?" And at first I was like, "Fine, he seems fine." And I changed the subject. But she kept circling back to it, and eventually I started sort of free-associating about it, and well, I don't know. Maybe I am more conflicted about Mom dating than I thought I was.

Anyway, after all that, the hour was up. But I do want to try to talk about the house stuff next week.

Thursday, May 21, 10:26 p.m.

Arthur came to dinner again. While he was there, I thought a lot about what Dr. Clyde had said, about my underlying animosity toward him and protectiveness toward my mom. But strange to say, he's just such a pleasant guy. It's hard to stay focused on that stuff when he's around. In fact, I kind of like when he comes by because it makes the house seem less spooky. Just me, Mom, and Logan in that big house . . . I don't know, it becomes tense. Sometimes I feel like we don't even know how to talk to each other anymore. But when Arthur is there, it smooths things over.

Although I don't know if Logan's feelings are the same as mine. Logan's a lot more withdrawn around him, which is weird, because Logan has always been such an outgoing kid. But I guess I can't really blame him. I mean, this must be hard

for him. And it's not like Logan's rude or anything, he just . . .
doesn't really laugh at Arthur's jokes, and looks like his mind is
elsewhere, even when Arthur is going out of his way to engage
him. I don't know, Logan's a funny kid. I'm sure he'll get over
it, though.

Wow, so was I ever wrong about the spiders.

The good news is that the flies have probably not been eating the spiders.

The bad news is . . . so inexpressibly horrifying that I don't know if I can even write it down.

Of course, Logan—my baby brother/science mentor—isn't bothered at all by it. He called me into his room after school today as I was walking past on my way downstairs. I hadn't been in there in ages. Thanks to that horrible buzzing noise, I've just been avoiding it since the night of his seizure. But he called to me, so, holding my breath, I opened the door and went in.

Instantly I had to press a palm to my forehead to calm the cacophony inside. "Jeez, Logan, how can you stand to sleep in here?"

But he just gave me a quizzical look, like he had no clue what I was talking about. Apparently he had dropped a comic book or something behind his dresser, and he needed help shifting it so he could get back there.

I got on the other side and we both gave a mighty heave, moving the old oak dresser about a foot away from the wall. Logan grabbed his comic book and we were about to shove the thing back into place when I stopped him.

"Look at that," I said. "The floor under the dresser is darker than the rest of the wood. It's totally discolored."

"So?" said Logan, the correct care and maintenance of hardwood floors not being a major area of interest for him, I guess.

"It's weird," I said. "We just brought this dresser from California, right? It's not like it's been sitting here 100 years. I wonder if the varnish from the dresser has been seeping off or something."

It didn't sound like a very convincing explanation, even to me, but I couldn't think of a better one. Shaking my head a little to stave off that annoying buzzing sound, I bent down to press my fingers to the darkened wood. I wanted to see if it felt sticky or wet at all, but about half an inch from contact, I froze.

Because the dark spot on the floor was moving. The whole patch, just . . . writhing and undulating. Holding my breath, I leaned down to look closer, and the whole thing is like a mass of teeny tiny little spiders crawling all over each other until they look like one solid organism.

And when I say tiny, I mean it. Each one was about the size of a pinhead, maybe slightly bigger. From a distance you couldn't really see them at all. But up close . . . Christ, I can still see that seething mass whenever I close my eyes. My vision got all gray at the edges, and all I could think was that those tiny spiders could be anywhere, could be under me, could be crawling all over me. I got up and ran down the stairs and outside, and I didn't stop until I reached a coffee shop downtown.

It's getting late now, and I really better go home. But I don't know how I'm going to set foot back in that house unless I somehow block what I've seen from my mind forever.

Therapy again. I tried a little harder to direct the conversation this time. It's weird. You go in there totally planning to talk about one thing, and then find yourself talking about something totally different. And it's not like Dr. Clyde is forcing me or anything. In fact, she hardly talks at all during the session. But having her there makes me realize I have stuff to say that I didn't even know I was thinking about. Magic!

This time I tried at least. At the beginning she asked me if there was anything in particular I wanted to talk about, and I was like, YES. It's about the house. And I was all proud of myself for bringing it up all directly like that, but then I wasn't sure where to go with it. I just felt so awkward telling her about the stuff that has happened, just because . . . well, damn, a lot of it sounds kind of dumb if you're not there, experiencing it.

Too many jars of tomato sauce in the cupboard? A bag of veggies that disappears and reappears mysteriously? Glitchy cell phone service? This stuff wouldn't even make the cut in a Scooby-Doo script. I tried to tell her about it, but even though she didn't say anything, I just got the feeling that she wasn't really buying it. Like this wasn't what she wanted to hear. But shouldn't therapy be about what's bothering *me* rather than what she wants to hear? I don't know, she's the professional. Maybe she knows better than I do.

Anyway, part of it was her nonengagement with what I was saying, and part of it was maybe just me hearing myself talk, and hearing how silly it all sounded. So we've got some flies and spiders and stuff—what old house doesn't? It's gross, but it's not supernatural. And everyone's got a million stories they can tell you about some time their cell phone screwed up.

But then I remembered the stuff with Logan . . . That stuff is pretty messed up, right? So I told her about that, about the seizure (in the middle of telling her I realized that obviously she already knows about that, and probably a lot of other stuff—she's Logan's doctor too), and about him playing video games that aren't there. And she didn't say anything. So then I told her about the letter, the duplicate letter he wrote. And I tried to really emphasize that it wasn't just a similar letter—it was identical.

I was so hoping that with that, I'd be able to break through her . . . I don't know, her professional reserve. I just wanted a genuine reaction out of her. Like a "Holy crap" or even just "That's kind of weird." Anything other than her medically approved "mmm-hmms" and "How did that make you feels." But I got a lot of that. And finally I was just like, no, how does that make *you* feel? I mean, isn't that strange? How would you explain it? All I want is some kind of explanation for it. For all this stuff.

But Dr. Clyde kept evading my question, and finally she was like, "Look, we're not here to talk about Logan. We're here to talk about you. Logan's problems are Logan's, and while they do affect you, I'm concerned that you are using his issues to deflect this conversation away from your own feelings."

When she said that . . . I had to sit with it a while. Because . . . I couldn't deny that when she put it that way, it made a lot of sense. Is that what I've been doing all along? Just putting all this on Mom and Logan because I'm scared to look at myself?

So then she asked me if there might be a reason I was directing the conversation toward Logan. Was there something going on in my relationship with him that was troubling me? And I told her obviously I am worried about him. And she just "mmm-hmm"d and nodded and looked . . . unconvinced. What's up with that? I hate that the most about therapy, I think. Like I can tell she is thinking something, but since she never says it, I can't confront her about it without looking crazy and paranoid. But the way her face looked . . . I could swear she thought that I had some, like, secret anger toward Logan. Which is such bullshit! I love Logan. I just want him to be okay again.

But then again, maybe that's not what Dr. Clyde was thinking at all. Maybe I just projected that onto her because I'm worried that there's something dark inside me. I don't know. Therapy is supposed to help you figure out and resolve the issues in your life, isn't it? But I feel like it's just making everything even more complicated.

I wonder if anyone's shrink has ever actually made them crazy.

WEDNESDAY, MAY 27, 6:10 A.M.

So I woke up this morning to a fantastic smell wafting through the house, like smoked bacon or something. I ran downstairs to find Arthur sitting at the kitchen table with a cup of coffee and a book. I asked him what was cooking and he cocked an eyebrow at me.

"Nothing," he says. "Just coffee . . . sorry."

So I'm thinking it must be a neighbor or something. I'm like, "Do you smell that? Like someone's having a barbecue or . . ."

That's when he gives me a smile that doesn't seem to have much humor behind it. "That's not food," he says. "That's fire. They're doing controlled burns all over the area right now."

"Oh right," I say. "To prevent wildfires."

And he's like, "Kind of. That may be a little optimistic."

"You think there will be a wildfire this year?" I say, and he laughs.

"There are wildfires every year. It's just a question of how bad. And this year looks like it might be pretty bad."

"How do you know?"

"We didn't get enough snow this winter."

"You mean sometimes there's more?"

He laughed again. This place is so weird. At least it smells nice, though.

THURSDAY, MAY 28, 10:27 P.M.

I forgot to mention before that Dr. Clyde did try to help me feel better about the house. She didn't ignore my concerns completely, in all fairness. I had mentioned the horrible ringing sound that seems to come from Logan's room, but maybe comes from inside of me. Toward the end of the session she brought it up and asked me if I might want to try some simple exercises that might help make the noise go away. And I was like, HELL YEAH, why didn't you offer me that in the first place?

So yeah, it's just really simple stuff. Like phrases to repeat to myself or visualize while I'm falling asleep, mostly. It seemed a little babyish, to be honest, but I've been doing it the past couple of nights, and you know what? The sound does seem to have faded a bit, to the point where I don't notice it unless I am listening for it. And I have been sleeping better, and getting along better with Mom. And I haven't even had any problem with Logan. So . . . I don't know. Maybe there is something to this therapy crap. Who knew?

Okay, scratch that. Shit. I don't even . . .

Okay. Deep breaths. This morning I woke up feeling awesome, well rested, and prepared for my bio test today. Mom was making pancakes, and Logan was chattering about some field trip. It was a good morning. Everyone was being normal.

But as we were getting our school stuff together in front of the door, I happened to notice something in Logan's bag. It was a letter. And I just got this pit in my stomach, because . . . who would Logan be writing to? He's a 12-year-old kid. He doesn't exactly have a lot of snail mail correspondents. So it had to be another letter to Dad. And I just couldn't help wondering, was it the same thing again? Was it normal, or was he at it again? I just had to know. And somehow, before I even consciously formed the thought, I took the letter out of his bag when he wasn't looking and put it in mine.

I know! It was a shitty thing to do. But I am worried about him, I really am, no matter what Dr. Clyde says. Besides, the letter could be like . . . evidence. Something tangible, that isn't just me blabbing about stuff I might completely be making up. And anyway, the ironic thing is that once Logan noticed it was missing, he probably wouldn't even think to blame me because so much random stuff goes missing in our house these days. He'd probably just assume it was our friendly ghosts. Ha.

I could hardly breathe the whole way into school. But the minute I sat down in homeroom, I got the letter out and ripped it open. My eyes scanned the first few lines, and instantly I knew. It was the *same* letter.

But there *was* something different this time—some of the words were crossed out. But not like, just a line through them, or a bit of a scribble, like a normal person might do. Someone—Logan, I guess—had gone over each crossed-out word probably a million times, scraping over and over with a ballpoint pen, until it made a deep indentation in the paper. And the words he had chosen seemed totally random. I can't figure it out at all, what he thought he was doing.

That's assuming there was any thought going on at all.

FRIDAY, MAY 29, 4:03 P.M.

Update . . . When I got home, I found Logan's last letter and compared them. Sure enough, they are word for word the same. And now I can see what words he was crossing out.

the
dead
will
bring
you
what
you
want
don't
want

sick
key
ana

What the hell.

Dear Dad,

Mom's making me write this letter. I mean, not that I mind writing to you, but she's making me write ~~a~~ letter by hand. The shrink has decrede that I'm not allowed to have screen time, so I have to email you the old fashioned way. I'm a little surprised to learn that the postal service isn't d~~ead~~ yet, but there are still people who ~~will~~ physicly ~~carry~~ paper with writing on it to your front door.

I'm getting excited about my science project. Have I told you about it? I'm trying to show what happens ~~when~~ you look at a really bright ~~light~~ for a while and then ~~look~~ at a white wall — like what the rods and cones are doing and stuff.

Do you think there's any chance you might be able to come for it? I don't know if you'd want to, but I think it will be interesting. I know ~~you're~~ busy, but I bet Paige would be really happy to see you. And I would be too.

By the way, have you been getting my gaming magazines? I don't know what happened to the subscription wh~~en we~~ moved but there's a review of the new Aeon of Strife that I want to check out. It's supposed to be sick.

Sorry if my ~~handwriting~~ writing is hard to read, it really never occurred to me that penmanship was going to be an issue in my life. I can't wait to get back to a ~~key~~board.

Well, it's almost morning and I'm starving. The ban~~ana~~ in the fruitbowl is calling to me. Write back soon!

Love,
Logan

SATURDAY, MAY 30, 3:23 P.M.

God, my eyes are killing me. How do people live like this? It's worse than allergies. Worse than that sandstorm, even. I woke up this morning and my eyes were *stinging* and I couldn't figure out why. My throat was burning too, so I thought, am I getting a cold? Strep? Then I looked out my windows as I was getting dressed, and the light looked . . . weird. Kind of golden, like sunset, even though it was nine in the morning.

Arthur stopped by for lunch and told us about the fires—all this golden haze means that somewhere out there, the fields and forests are burning.

"Out there?" I said. "What about the town? Will it . . . ?"

The rest of the thought is too scary to finish, but Arthur smiled and shook his head. "No, they're really far away now," he said. "Hundreds of miles, in fact, but the wind is so strong, it sweeps the ash and debris over to us. But there's no danger here. Not now, anyway."

I wanted to know how it started. A cigarette butt? A campfire? But Arthur says it's not that simple, it could be almost anything. Sometimes it starts with a lightning strike. Sometimes the farm machinery shoots off a spark from metal rubbing metal. And that's all it takes. The next thing you know, the fields are blazing.

TUESDAY, JUNE 2, 8:27 P.M.

So all week I've been looking forward—if you can call it that—
to my session with Dr. Clyde so I could show her this new
evidence. I figured, there was no way she could deflect this, no
way she could argue that everything in the house was just a
symptom of my own psychological distress.

Guess I have a lot to learn about psychiatrists.

I didn't even wait for her to ask me how my week went, or
if there was anything I needed to talk about. I took out the letter right away and handed it to her without a word. She tried to
ask me a lot of questions before she even looked at it—trying to
regain control of the session, I guess. But I was insistent. I just
kept telling her to read it. Finally she did.

"Okay," she said when she was done. "Do you want to tell me
something about this?"

"It's Logan. Don't you see? He's doing it again. Only it's even worse now. Look at those words, look at—"

But Dr. Clyde wouldn't listen. She just kept trying to get me to calm down, to sit down. Eventually I did. "Paige," she said once I had stopped ranting, "we need to talk about this. I'm growing increasingly concerned about you."

That took me by surprise.

"About me?" I said. "But I'm showing you . . . it's not me, it's Logan! Or really . . . I don't think it's Logan, either. This isn't like him. Something has gotten inside of him. Something is making him do this. It's possessed him the same way it possessed my phone, the way it moves stuff around in our kitchen, making us all think the others are crazy . . . or that we are." Dr. Clyde didn't say anything, just looked at me with big, serious eyes. "That's what you think, isn't it?" I said. "You think I'm nuts." I couldn't help laughing a little to myself, though there wasn't any humor in it. "Of course, that's what people pay shrinks for, isn't it? To tell us that we're nuts. That's your training. How are you ever going to see anything else? But think about it, Dr. Clyde—how can this be about me? *Logan* did this, not me. How can that make me crazy?"

Dr. Clyde hesitated a long time before answering. "Paige," she said at last, "no one is calling you crazy. But it's clear you have been under a lot of stress lately, and there are latent issues you aren't ready to deal with. Do you know anything about repression?"

I stared blankly at her, though rage was building in my chest.

She starts to explain repression to me, speaking slowly as if I'd never heard of the concept. She explains that repression is when we have thoughts or feelings that we think we're not supposed to. The thoughts cause guilt and shame, so we protect ourselves by pushing those thoughts down into our unconscious so we don't have to deal the them. We try to keep only happy, positive thoughts in our heads. But it doesn't work for long. You can push the scary stuff down, you can hide it, but you can't make it go away—not like that, anyway. And the more you push it down, the harder it pushes back. It starts coming up again, burbling to the surface, but in different ways. Then she says, "Sometimes we see very strange behaviors manifesting themselves. Stuff that doesn't seem to make any sense at all. But when you look at it at the level of the unconscious, it all starts to make sense. The unconscious has its own logic, and it can't be denied."

That last part got to me. I hated the way she could say things so clearly without ever really saying them at all. I had to pin her down. "You're saying that's what's going on with Logan?" I asked. "That it's not a haunting or a spirit possession or whatever . . . that it's his own mind doing this to him?"

Again, Dr. Clyde didn't speak for a long moment. "Paige," she said at last, "I understand your concern for your brother. But remember what we talked about last week—about using him to hide from your own issues. I want you to think, Paige. Think hard about where this letter came from."

"What do you mean? I told you, I got it out of his bag. I read it at school, and then—" But then something clicked. She never said anything, but I looked into her face and read everything there I needed to know. "You think it was me," I said, reeling from the shock. "You think I crossed out these words. Hell, maybe you think I wrote them in the first place."

"Paige," she said, "I want you to think about where all this negative energy is coming from. The animosity you feel toward your brother. Is it because you see your father in him? Does it have to do with your mother's new boyfriend? Acknowledging those feelings and working through them is the only way you're going to—"

But I didn't stay to hear the end of her psychobabble. I had to get out of there.

WEDNESDAY, JUNE 3, 12:05 A.M.

Dr. Clyde has gotten under my skin. Now that she has put this idea in my head, I can't stop wondering if she's right. What if it's all in my head? I guess that's what I wanted to hear from the beginning, right? That I had some kind of mental issue that was causing all this, and it could be diagnosed and treated and cured. But I didn't expect it to be like this . . . I always thought of mental illness as like other kinds of illness. Like, you're this complete, whole, normal person, but then cancer or the flu or an infection comes along and messes you up, but you're still you. I guess I pictured mental stuff the same way. Like a film that is covering your normal brain, making you see things funny, and you just need someone to scrape it away to be all right again.

But what Dr. Clyde is suggesting . . . what if this isn't an illness that happened to me? What if this is all the "me" there is? And I do things I don't remember, and I . . . *feel* things I don't even recognize. Maybe my whole life, I've had something inside of me . . . something crazy, something wrong, something *bad* . . . and I kept it hidden from everyone. Even myself. What if the normal me, the sane me that I think I know, that everyone around me knows—what if that's the film? And what if something in my life—the divorce, or living in this house, or my sessions with Dr. Clyde—is now scraping it away?

I don't know if I want to see what's underneath.

WEDNESDAY, JUNE 3, 3:55 P.M.

I woke up this morning to find the yards in our neighborhood under a blanket of snow. It's June! Even in Idaho, that seemed excessive. There was something odd about it, though. It covered the neighborhood, but not the fields behind the house, which are still green. And it doesn't sparkle.

Turns out it's not snow but cottonwood fluff. Arthur explained, and said it's like this every year. You have to watch out for it because it ignites so easily. Ash from a cigarette butt could wind up setting the whole town aflame. Especially with the dry weather we've had lately.

It's weird, though. Where did it all come from so suddenly? I never even knew we had cottonwood trees, and then one day there is this fluffy white stuff all over everything. I touched it and it stuck all over my fingers and clothes. Gross, but also kind of cool.

Bug update: I'm still unsettled about the spiders I saw in Logan's room. Let's hope they are just a fluke in Logan's room, and not under every piece of furniture in this house. In any case, I am not checking under the others, science be damned.

The flies I was keeping in that jar seemed to have finally kicked it. They're all lying feet up on the bottom of the jar. The ones downstairs are still going strong, so I guess that at least tells me these flies do need food to survive. I hadn't fed them in ages. (Don't tell Mom. It was really more accident than any deliberate plan to torture them.)

I feel slightly bad, but mostly good that these flies follow natural laws and aren't superhuman. Superfly? Wait, no, that means something different.

WEDNESDAY, JUNE 3, 4:07 P.M.

Uhhhh, scratch that! I picked up the jar to toss it in the trash, and suddenly they all started buzzing around again. That's . . . freaky.

Now I'm not sure what to do with them. Guess I'll leave them on the desk and keep ~~staring at them in horror~~ studying them?

FRIDAY, JUNE 5, 5:30 A.M.

Logan had another seizure tonight.

I don't understand it. I thought he was doing better. We did everything Dr. Clyde said—stopped the Ritalin, took away his video games . . . Shouldn't he be better now? But then again, did I really think he was better? For a while he seemed to be sleeping a bit, but lately I've seen him up in the middle of the night plenty of times. And those letters . . . I don't know what to think anymore. Dr. Clyde had me half-convinced that I crossed out all those words to create that message. But if it really was Logan all along . . .

And I can't even tell if this is just a medical issue, or if it's something more. Something . . . different. But what would that even be?

I was lying in bed tonight, listening to the usual shrieks and howls of the wind blowing through the house, and then suddenly the wind died and it was eerily silent in the house.

I looked at my clock and it was a little after 3 a.m. I lay in bed for a while, trying to figure out what was bothering me—if it was a dreaming or waking sensation—and then I realized . . . it felt like the whole house was moving. Or . . . *swaying*. Almost like it was dancing. The only thing I'd ever experienced that was similar was earthquakes back in California, but Idaho doesn't get earthquakes. And this felt different, anyway. More rhythmic.

After a bit, the rocking stopped, but I couldn't go back to sleep. I could feel the vibrations from Logan's room building in my bones, and I decided to check on him. I got out of bed and went to his room, but his bed was empty. I stood in the center of the room for a while in the uncanny stillness of the night, trying not to look at those strange symbols in the walls, trying to ignore the building tension emanating from the room itself. The sound was even worse now. I could feel it creeping through my whole body, making my bones and organs vibrate painfully. And in my head . . . what had once sounded kind of like a person screaming now sounded like an army of voices, some talking, some babbling, some crying and moaning in agony. No one else had ever confessed to hearing it, but even so—was it any wonder Logan had trouble sleeping in here?

I left the room to go look for him, sure that I would find him parked in front of the TV again, but he wasn't. Instead I found him in the kitchen. There was bread laid out on the counter, and jars of peanut butter and jelly. And Logan was twitching on the floor.

I screamed and Mom came running. A couple of minutes later, Arthur was there too. I looked at him strangely, and Mom made some comment about her not wanting him to drive all the way home so late at night. At the time, I was too distracted by Logan to make much of it, but I guess this means Mom has taken their relationship to the next level. Ew. Can't wait to see what Dr. Clyde makes of that.

Anyway, Mom called 911 and an ambulance came and took them both to the hospital, leaving me alone with Arthur. Arthur seemed pretty spooked, but I could tell he wanted to reassure me. He was like, wow, that was . . . something. But don't worry, your brother is in good hands now. The doctors will look after him, and he'll be fine. I just nodded mutely.

Arthur said, "You should go back to bed," and I nodded, but I didn't move. As if sleep were even a remote possibility. Arthur caught on quick. "You're not going back to bed, are you?" I shook my head. "You want some coffee?" He waited for another nod, then put the pot on.

"You know he's going to be okay, right? The doctors will look after him, and they'll figure out what's going on." I didn't respond. I appreciated his efforts to make me feel better, but I didn't have it in me to play along. Arthur sat down in the chair opposite me. "You know," he said, "I've got a cousin with epilepsy. It's scary, but it's not that big a deal, really. He just has to take some precautions, some medication . . . but he's fine, he's still the same guy."

"This is different," I said without thinking. I hadn't really meant to spill the beans to Arthur. He's a nice guy, but I figured he didn't need to know all the grotesque details of our life here. Anyway, I expected him to brush it off the way most people have—like Mom and Dad and Dr. Clyde. To tell me, sure, it feels different to you, because you're so close to the situation, but you're just a kid, you don't understand, blah blah. But he didn't.

"Different how?"

"This isn't epilepsy."

"Well," he said, "I guess we can't know anything for sure yet. Sometimes there are other causes for seizures, but the doctors will—"

"The doctors won't be able to fix this." Arthur didn't say anything, he just looked at me. I decided to give it my best shot and explain myself. "There's something really wrong," I said, speaking carefully, not sure how much I was ready to reveal. "Not with Logan. With something else." Still, Arthur didn't speak, but his open expression seemed to urge me to go on. Not like Dr. Clyde's silences, where I always seemed to be able to read what she wanted or expected me to say. Like he was really listening. "I think it's the house."

"The house?" he said. "This house?"

"You haven't noticed anything?"

"Well, it's old. Kind of. Old for white people. If you come down to the reservation someday, I can show you stuff with a lot more history than this house."

"Is any of that stuff . . . haunted?" Immediately I felt dumb for using the word. "I mean," I tried again, "do you think any of that old stuff ever"—I reached for a phrase I'd heard my mom use—"accrues energy?"

"Energy," he repeated with a frown. I don't think I'd ever seen him frown before, but it seemed more thoughtful than disapproving. "Yeah," he said, "I think I know what you mean. But I wouldn't say haunted. The tradition I was raised with says that the spirits of our ancestors are with us all the time, everywhere—but it's nothing to be afraid of. They watch over us and protect us. It can be a great comfort to know that our loved ones never truly leave us."

And now I definitely know what he and my mom have in common. How is it so easy for everyone to believe in happy, peaceful hauntings? I'm sick of people trying to reassure me that I have nothing to fear from the dead. It's all very well to *say* that the dead bear us no ill will, but that's not always what it looks like.

I decided to try to get Arthur to see this point. "What if some of these spirits aren't so nice?" I asked him. "What if they don't seem protective? What if they seem . . . threatening?" And so, as we finished our cups of coffee, and he poured us more, I let loose with all the little things that I had noticed since we moved in. By the time I finished, it was starting to get light out, and I could hear birds.

Arthur was quiet for a moment, staring down into his coffee. "I've heard some stories," he said at last. "Unfriendly spirits, some people say. Other people call them demons. I had a cousin—a different cousin—who went through something similar with her whole family. They live up on Sundown Heights, and everyone says there are spirits up there. The spirits live on the hillside and pass from house to house, if people give them a chance to come in. They say you have to close your curtains at night or they'll watch you through the window. Don't cry at night or they'll hear you and come in. And if you eat with the windows open, they'll come in for the food and when they can't get it, they wreak all kinds of havoc. She told me one night she looked out the kitchen window and saw a little girl's hand in a frilly white glove, just sticking out of the dirt."

"Jesus. Was she scared?"

"What do you think? Her first instinct was to burn the whole place down and never look back. People used to do that more in the old days—a good burn will purify a place like nothing else. You come back next year to find mushrooms and berries instead of creepy undead babies. But we don't have enough land anymore to just walk away from a fire, so instead my grandfather came over to do a cleansing."

"Did that work?"

"Sure it did. He's a tribal elder, and when he speaks, everyone listens. Even the dead." I didn't say anything, but the look on my face must have spoken volumes. "Do you want me to see if he'll come?"

I couldn't speak or even nod at this offer, but tears of relief rolled down my cheeks.

SATURDAY, JUNE 6, 10:33 A.M.

These flies are really freaking me out, man. I'll be so sure they are all dead, and then I come back from brunch an hour later and they are flying around like nothing's the matter.

They look pretty healthy now. I kind of have another experiment in mind, though. Hmm, let's see how this goes.

Okay, that . . . did not make me feel any better. Basically, I took one of the flies out of the jar and wacked the hell out of it with my history textbook. Then I put it back in the jar. I know, that's weird, but I wanted to see if it would come back to life.

It did not. The other flies, however, immediately landed on the bottom of the jar and are now standing in a circle around it. What is this, an insect funeral? This is too strange.

SATURDAY, JUNE 6, 10:49 A.M.

Left to take a shower, and when I got back, the dead fly was gone. I can't figure out what happened to it.

Did it regenerate and come back to life? To be honest, I'm not totally sure how many flies were in the jar in the first place, so I'm not sure if it's flying around now or not. But I don't think so. I really don't know what the hell happened.

~~Okay I am pretty sure the other flies ate it but I don't want to think about that.~~

MONDAY, JUNE 8, 10:15 P.M.

Chloe came over today. Logan is still in the hospital for observation, and Mom is with him. I guess I just wasn't thrilled about being alone in the house, so I invited her over, supposedly to celebrate the beginning of summer vacation. I don't think I managed to look convincingly celebratory.

Even with her there, I found I didn't really want to be inside. It feels oppressive. So we sat on the porch, watching the cottonwood fluff drift around the neighborhood. I still can't get over how weird it is—not just a bit of fluff here and there, but sheets of it on every flat surface, laid out like quilt batting. It's hard to get used to.

After a bit, Chloe got bored and decided she wanted to harass Raph. I told her I didn't think that was a great idea.

"Why?" she said. "I thought you guys hung out. Wasn't your mom, like, planning your nuptials?"

"Yeah," I said, thinking awkwardly of my last meeting with him, in that darkened apartment filled with boxes. "Pretty sure the wedding is off." I told her about Raph's strange behavior and his sinister warnings, but I don't think she really got the full extent of it. Somehow, when I speak, people always hear what they want to hear. I had hardly finished the story before she was bounding down the porch stairs toward his door.

"What are you doing?"

"Going to see Raph."

"But—"

"The way I see it," she said over her shoulder, "there are two possibilities. Either that last time was a fluke, and he's fine now, and so it can't do any harm to see him."

"Or?"

"Or . . . he's not okay. He's got some kind of problems. In which case it's basically a good deed to check up on him, isn't it?"

I turned this over in my head. There was certainly a logic to her words, but still . . . I remembered his face last time, when he had told me to stay away from him. As if he was . . . not exactly *threatening* me. Warning me, maybe. But I still couldn't make any sense of it. What could he possibly be warning me about? Did he think *he* had caused Logan's seizures? Or all the other weird stuff in the house? That seemed unlikely. I don't know why, but I was pretty sure that if there was something up with the house, it was something dead or supernatural causing it. Not a perfectly healthy college boy (a.k.a. a semi-healthy ex–college boy). Still, it seemed rude to intrude on him again, after he had been so anxious around me last time. On the other hand, I *was* curious about what was going on with him. I hesitated a moment longer, then followed Chloe to his door.

Chloe knocked confidently, and Raph opened it almost immediately with a smile on his face, as if he had been expecting us. Or expecting *someone*. His smile fell a bit when he saw us, and he ran a hand through his hair. "Oh," he said. "You guys. What's up?"

I expected Chloe to speak, but she seemed unaccountably tongue-tied, given her boldness only minutes earlier.

"We just, you know, wanted to say hi," I tried, smiling nervously. "And check in on—I mean, see how you're doing. I mean, say how are you. How are you?" Ugh, will I ever not babble like an idiot in front of this boy?

Raph nodded knowingly. "So this is what, a welfare check? Want to see if I've started carving the names of demons into all the walls of my apartment?"

"Oh my God," said Chloe, finding her voice. "Have you? That would be so metal."

Raph stepped aside and extended an arm, inviting us in. Chloe went in first and spun around, taking in all the walls. "Oh," she said, sounding disappointed. I followed her and saw what she saw: totally normal walls, nothing spooky carved into them at all. What's more, the place looked really different from the last time I had been there. For one thing, the curtains and blinds were open, and the sun was shining in. Also, all the boxes were gone, and the surfaces all around the apartment were neat and clear.

"What happened to all the boxes?" I asked. For a moment, I flashed back to my last session with Dr. Clyde, and was struck with a cold panic that I had imagined my whole last interaction with Raph. But no, I had taken that weird pamphlet back with me, and even shown it to Chloe. I couldn't have just made all that up. In any case, Raph dissipated my fears with his next comment.

"Gone," he said. "We took them back to the library."

"We?" said Chloe.

"I did," he said, blushing a little. "I mean, someone helped me. A friend helped me. It was a lot of boxes."

"You have a friend?" said Chloe incredulously, which seemed kind of mean. But it was true that I had never seen anyone come to visit Raph, other than his mom and the delivery drivers. Raph's expression showed that he felt the slight, but he didn't respond to it.

"The place is a lot clearer now, isn't it? It was . . ." He laughed awkwardly. "It was annoying, having all those boxes everywhere."

"What were you doing with them?" I asked.

"Just . . . research," he said.

"Did you find what you were looking for?" said Chloe.

"No," he said.

"Oh," she said. "Sorry."

"No," he said. "It's a good thing. I mean, it's . . . sometimes, when you're doing research, you're trying to prove something. A hypothesis. But if you don't find evidence, that's good too. Sometimes even better."

Chloe and I exchanged a glance. It would be an exaggeration to say Raph was acting *normal*—he was still talking in riddles and not making a hell of a lot of sense, for one. But at least he seemed . . . happy. And his apartment certainly looked more normal. All in all, the signs pointed to an improvement in his mental health. So why did I feel so edgy?

"But it still means you were wrong, doesn't it?" said Chloe.

"Yeah," said Raph. "But sometimes wrong is exactly what you want to be." And he let out a slightly unhinged giggle.

"You were researching Pronoica," said Chloe.

She had hardly said the words before Raph's expression shifted. The happiness and relief exchanged for a flash of that haunted look I had seen on his face last time we spoke. "How did you know about that?" he asked sharply.

"I'm sorry," I said, shooting daggers at Chloe for selling me out. "That was me. I happened to pick up one of the pamphlets you had lying around last time and I showed it to her."

Raph knitted his brows and his face darkened again. "You shouldn't have done that," he said, and I was revisited by the chill I had felt during our previous conversation. But he seemed to catch himself and he relaxed his face as he said, "I mean, all that stuff belongs to the library. You can't just walk off with it."

I told him I'd bring it back, but he seemed more interested in Chloe now. "What do you know about Pronoica?" he asked.

She shrugged. "Not much. Just that it was some kooky cult, basically. Except, it wasn't even real . . . The whole thing was done through the mail, right? My grandpa told me once that the reason the post office in this town is so big is because of Pronoica. That guy, Frank Williamson—they called him the Mail Order Messiah. He used to take out advertisements in the backs of magazines, promising power and enlightenment to any sucker who sent him ten dollars."

"And people fell for that?" I asked.

Raph shifted his gaze away from us. "You sure they were suckers?"

I couldn't help laughing. "What, so you're saying Williamson sent people supernatural powers through the mail?"

Raph rubbed his knuckles against his scalp thoughtfully. "You guys want some tea? My mom just brought me a new teakettle, and now I drink tea constantly." Without waiting for our answer, he ran the kettle under the kitchen tap. It did not escape my notice that he'd changed the subject again. Chloe looked like she was going to ask him more about Pronoica, but I shot her a warning glance. We let him chatter on about tea varieties for the rest of our visit.

TUESDAY, JUNE 9, 9:25 A.M.

God, my eyes are waiting killing me. How do people live like this? It's worse than allergies. Worse for than that sandstorm, even. I woke up this you morning and my eyes were *stinging* and I couldn't figure out why. My to throat was burning too, so I thought, am I getting a recognize cold? Strep? Then I looked out my windows as I was getting dressed, and the light looked . . . weird. Kind of golden, like a sunset, even though it was nine that in the morning.

Arthur stopped by for lunch and invisible told us about the fires—all this golden haze means that somewhere out there, the fields though and forests are burning.

"Out there?" I asked. "What about the town? Will it . . . ?"

The rest of the thought is too powerful scary to finish, but Arthur smiled and shook his presence head. "No, they're really far away now," he said. "Hundreds of miles, in fact, but the wind is so strong, it sweeps the ash and debris over to us they. But there's no danger here. Not now, anyway."

I want to are know how it started. A cigarette butt? A camp-fire? But Arthur says it's not that simple, it could be almost anything. Sometimes it starts with a lightning pregnant strike. Sometimes the farm machinery with shoots off a spark from spiritual metal rubbing metal. And that's all it takes. The next thing you know, the fields are blazing power.

TUESDAY, JUNE 9, 3:46 P.M.

Another session with Dr. Clyde today. A weird one. I told her about Logan's most recent seizure, again forgetting that she must already know. I wanted to challenge her on that—obviously the seizures are in his head, not in mine. So why should she assume I'm making up all the other stuff? But I didn't really make any headway there. She just kept asking me how I felt about it, and when I said I was worried, she seemed dissatisfied, and asked the same thing again in a different way. Like she wants a different answer. But what? It's almost like she wants me to say I hate Logan or something, which is NOT true. But even if it were . . . it's not like I can give him seizures. Can I? No, that's crazy. Even by the standards of someone who thinks she lives in a haunted house, that's nuts.

I tried to shore up my position by telling her about Arthur

and how I had told the whole story to him, a real, responsible adult, and he had believed me. At least, he seemed to. But that took Dr. Clyde off in a whole other direction. She wanted to know how I felt about learning Arthur was spending the night. I was like, I think we have a bigger issue on our hands here . . . ? But she didn't want to let it go. Shrinks, man—they have a one-track mind.

So then I brought up Raph, I'm not sure why. I guess for another example of inexplicable stuff going on in the house that can't possibly be my fault, or my imagination. But that's when things got weird. I had mentioned him to her a couple of times before, but just as "the cute boy who lives downstairs." I mean, she asked me about boys directly during our first session, and it's not like I have anything else going on. So I mentioned him, but she didn't seem terribly interested, and it's not like I really wanted to talk about it either.

Anyway, I mentioned him again this time. I think I said, "Raph is acting weird too," and I was about to go into his sort of odd behavior the last couple of times I saw him, though I figured she wouldn't make much of it. He's been weird but not, like, supernaturally weird. But I didn't even get to tell her anything more because she stopped me there.

"Who?" she said.

I said, "Raph, the guy who lives downstairs. His mom is—"

"That's the college boy you mentioned?"

"Yeah, he lives in—"

"And you say he's behaving strangely?"

"Well, kind of, but I don't have much to—"

And that's when Dr. Clyde interrupted me again, to ask exactly what Raph had done. Which was weird, because she never interrupts. Talking to a shrink isn't like chatting with a friend or your mom or whatever. Their whole point is to let you keep talking forever and ever and ever, in hopes that you'll stumble into something interesting. Or revealing. Or I guess if I want to be cynical, maybe they let you talk and talk because it kills the time and runs down the hour, so they get paid without doing any actual work. But either way, I had definitely noticed that Dr. Clyde only ever talked if I've been silent for a good long pause. Usually at least a few seconds, sometimes maybe a whole minute. And she definitely never interrupted. So why was she doing it now? What had I said to get her so worked up? Nothing, really. Nothing except . . .

"Do you know Raph?" I said.

Dr. Clyde was silent a moment. Then she said, "No, I don't. But even if I did, Paige, you know the rules about confidentiality. Of course I couldn't tell you."

"That's a yes, isn't it?"

"No. That's a no."

"What do you know about him?"

"I don't know anything, Paige. I'm only responding to what you're saying, what you've told me, and what I notice in your body language. But I think . . . I'm going to advise you to stay away from this young man."

"But you don't even know him."

"It's for your own good. Stay away from him, Paige. Trust me."

WEDNESDAY, JUNE 10, 2:57 P.M.

I was so disturbed by what Dr. Clyde said yesterday that I completely forgot Arthur's grandfather was coming by today. Luckily, he texted me when they were on their way, so I was able to clean up a bit and not be completely taken by surprise. I checked the cupboards for any cookies I could serve with tea, but honestly, I had no freaking idea how one is supposed to entertain a tribal elder.

The other thing that was weird was that Mom didn't know. I never mentioned it to her, but I guess I assumed Arthur would tell her. He apparently didn't—maybe he assumed the same thing of me—so I had to fill her in quickly as their car pulled up. I'm guessing a lot of moms in the world would have trouble with the idea of some old man coming to their house to recite mumbo jumbo, but since Mom is basically the queen of mumbo jumbo herself, she took it pretty well.

I watched out the window as the old man eased out of the car with some help from Arthur. He was wearing jeans and an orange fleece jacket, and he had long white hair with a cropped ponytail on the crown of his head. As he made his way toward the house, two little kids hopped out of the backseat and started chasing each other up and down the porch stairs.

"Quit it, guys," said Arthur over his shoulder as I met him at the front door, trying to clear a path through the slowly circling flies for them to walk through. "More cousins," he said to me. "I hope you don't mind. Pops likes to bring the little ones along to these things."

I nodded, but Pops apparently thought it needed more explanation. "The rituals are in danger of being forgotten," he said, his breath still coming a little heavy from the exertion of the stairs. "Ours is mostly an oral tradition, which means we need to be in the same place, repeating the same words together, or it will be lost."

Arthur smiled a little apologetically at the old man's words. "My brother is writing his dissertation on the Nez Perce language. A lot of the old stories are being written down, so they'll be more permanent now."

Pops gave him a sharp look. "Writing is good, but some things were not meant to be written down." Pops then turned to me and Mom and looked us over. "You're the ones who live here?" he said. "The ones who are visited by spirits?"

I looked up at Mom, not quite ready to say the words aloud to a complete stranger. She gave him a pleasant smile and nodded. "My son lives here too, but he's at a friend's house for the evening. Will that be all right?"

Pops waved a hand in her direction. "Sure," he said. "No big deal. Where do you want me to set up?"

Mom looked around a little uncertainly, then guided him toward the kitchen table. "I guess this will work," she said. As he began to set out his props, she continued. "Look, I'm not sure what my daughter told you, but you're not going to do anything . . . *unfriendly* to these spirits, are you? My philosophy is live and let live ("live and let haunt," I couldn't help muttering under my breath) and I, well, I don't want to toss anyone out, especially since they were here first. Exorcisms can be so . . . spiritually violent."

Pops raised his eyebrows at her. I wondered if he got this kind of speech from a lot of crazy ex-hippies, or if this was a first for him. "It's not an exorcism," he said impatiently. "Ceremonies like this one are really for the living, not the dead. This house cannot be blessed because it is blessed already by the spirits of the people who have lived here. This is only an acknowledgment of that blessing."

Mom nodded, satisfied with this explanation. Pops took a bag from Arthur and pulled out an iridescent shell about the size of a baseball mitt, and placed a dried-up fir branch inside. "Patosway," he said as he lit a match and held it to the branch. "It has many cleansing properties. And the fire acts as a purifying agent." The match went out.

"That's our ancestors' idea of a joke," he said with a gentle smile, and he lit another. That one, too, went out. He went through six matches, losing a little more of his good humor each time, until at last on the seventh he was able to light the branch. He blew out the flame and wafted the resulting smoke around the kitchen and toward the front hall. It smelled wonderful,

though it stung my eyes before it dissipated. The kids stood around the table, fidgeting and looking bored.

After a minute, Pops pulled out a shiny brass bell and rang it three times, using his whole arm to swing it back and forth. I was so focused on the sound, I almost didn't notice my cell phone buzz in my pocket. I reached in to turn it off. "Sorry," I said.

Pops cast me a dark look, but I noticed Mom and Arthur reach into pockets to turn their phones off right afterward.

Pops put down the bell and began reciting a long prayer in a strange but beautiful language. Before he was done, though, we heard another vibration. Pops froze, stopping the prayer. I looked at the other two, but they just shrugged. Pops cleared his throat and continued with his song, but before long he broke off again. "What is that?" he said.

"What?" said Mom.

"That . . . noise. Don't you hear it? Some kind of buzzing—"

"Oh," I said. "You hear that too? I thought I was the only one." The strange noise from Logan's room. I only occasionally notice it anymore, but that's not because it stopped. It's just become so ever-present that I tune it out these days, except when it gets really bad, or when I stop and focus on it. Which I try not to do.

Pops turned to the kids and said something in that strange language. They both stared at him blankly. "Arthur," he said in English, "take the kids outside."

"What?" said Arthur. "You sure?"

Pops only nodded, and Arthur shrugged and herded the kids toward the front door. Pops began his prayer again, his voice a little unsteady at first but gaining strength as he went. When he finished, he rang the bell again and began to sing in a rich, deep baritone. I'd closed my eyes to focus on the beautiful sound when I felt the vibration picking up, becoming more intense. Like the day of Logan's seizure, I could feel it building in my bones, my blood, twisting my organs. I opened my eyes to look at the old man, and I could see from the pinched expression on his face that he felt it too.

Then at that moment, the strange noise was drowned by the sound of every cell phone in the room going off. Or . . . not drowned, exactly. The ringtones and vibrations almost felt like they were ringing in sympathy with the buzzing crescendo.

"What the hell?" said Arthur as he grabbed the phone from his pocket. "I just turned this thing off."

The noise stopped suddenly. Not just the phones—the buzzing had stopped too, and an eerie stillness replaced it. Then Arthur's phone beeped twice, and we all jumped. Arthur picked it up and furrowed his brow at the screen. "That's weird," he said. "Pops, did you text me earlier? We've been together all day . . ."

"It's okay," said Mom. "Phones do that sometimes in this house. It happens to all of us."

For a moment, Pops just stared at her. Then he grabbed his bell and made for the door, moving much faster than he had seemed capable of earlier. I followed him out to the porch. "Wait," I called. "Where are you going?"

He was talking to Arthur. "Get the kids, we're leaving."

"You can't just go," I protested. "We need you. I thought you said you could help."

Pops turned and looked me in the eye, his countenance dark and fearful. "There's something really wrong here."

"Yeah," I said. "That's what I was trying to tell you. And you said—"

"I know what I said. Listen, I've been by this house loads of times. I've even been in it, back when it housed a businessman's association. It was fine then. But something has changed. There is something very bad here." He started down the stairs.

"Pops," said Arthur, "you came all this way, can't you just—"

The old man turned sharply. "No. This is outside my power. Most of the time people complain their house is haunted, and it's nothing. They get a bad feeling, maybe some dreams. I say a few words, and it goes away. That's not going to work here. This is bigger."

"What am I supposed to do, then?" I said.

"Beats me," replied the old man. "You're in trouble."

THURSDAY, JUNE 11, 10:00 A.M.

Looks like the fly experiment is officially over. Also, not sure if Mom will ever speak to me again.

She caught me murdering the rest of the flies with my history textbook. I tried to explain to her that it was for science, and that there was a good chance they would all come back to life in a few minutes, but she didn't want to hear it.

THURSDAY, JUNE 11, 4:00 P.M.

I made Chloe meet me downtown for coffee today. I had to tell her what Arthur's grandfather had said. I don't know what I was expecting. I think I was hoping for reassurance. I think I imagined her making a big joke out of it, laughing at the idea that I would fall for some old man's bogeyman story. Or that she would delve into the gothness of it, and become fascinated and obsessed and excited about the idea of anything legitimately supernatural, from beyond the grave. That would have been okay too, because if she was excited about it, then it couldn't really be that scary, could it?

But she didn't do either of those things. Instead she was silent for a long moment, looking at me with wide brown eyes, and with that look fixed on her face—the problem-solving one. Gradually her brows knotted as she focused more and more intensely on the problem. Then, just as I was starting to get seriously freaked out, she spoke.

"You have to talk to Raph."

I wasn't expecting that. "Right," I said. "Because that went so well the last couple of times."

"I'm serious, Paige. He knows something. Don't you see it? He's been hiding something from us this whole time. Something to do with his research project, with those boxes you saw, with that pamphlet you showed me, getting kicked out of school . . . What's his secret?"

At first I wanted to scoff. Weird as he was, something about Raph had always struck me as quite harmless. Sure, he had some stuff he didn't like to talk about, but who doesn't? But then I remembered . . .

"Dr. Clyde," I said. Chloe looked at me in confusion. "My shrink. She said something about Raph during my last session. Told me to stay away from him. And Raph said the same thing. Do you think he might have been one of her patients?"

"Not unlikely. It's a small town. I know three people who have been to see her. But if he is . . ."

"What?"

"Don't you see what that means? It means she knows stuff. It means he has told her stuff, stuff that he wouldn't tell anyone else. And now she's telling you to stay away from him."

I took a moment to absorb this.

"Paige," she said, "you have to go talk to him."

"Actually, doesn't it sound like I should stay as far away from him as possible?"

"Do you want to figure out what's going on in your house, or don't you? He's got the answer. I'm sure of it."

I shook my head, uncomfortable with this plan. "He always changes the subject. He doesn't like to talk about certain things, and . . . well, shouldn't I respect that?"

Chloe looked at me seriously. "We're not talking about a gambling problem, or his sex life. This is not the time for being polite. You heard the old man yourself—there is something sinister in your house. Something beyond our understanding, maybe beyond anyone's. And Raph could have the key. You have to talk to him."

FRIDAY, JUNE 12, 8:22 A.M.

Well, I put together a few more pieces of the puzzle last night.

Seeing how nervous and unconvinced I was during our coffee date, Chloe offered to come with me to Raph's place—perhaps to lend moral support, or more likely because she was afraid I'd chicken out. But I told her no. I love Chloe, but she has a way about her . . . You only have to see her status at school to know that she has a tendency to rub some people the wrong way. And Raph was hypersensitive under the best of circumstances. With people deliberately pushing at the things he had walled off and forbidden us to talk about . . . I had a feeling the situation could be volatile.

After dinner I steeled myself and headed down to the basement with no idea which version of Raph to expect. When he opened the door, I checked his face for clues. He seemed more calm, less manic than he had last time . . . and he didn't kick me out right away, which I took as a good sign. But stepping closer, I noticed his eyes were rimmed with red, and as he closed the door behind me, he wiped his nose on the back of his hand.

"Allergies?" I said.

"What?" said Raph. "Oh yeah. Spring's the worst. All that cottonwood fluff in the air . . ."

I stood in the middle of the room, looking around for any clue to what Raph knew. Any clue that would let me get out of there and mollify Chloe, without having to actually speak and reveal my mission. The apartment was not as crazy looking as it had been with the boxes everywhere, but it also didn't look as spic and span as it had the last time I had been here. Instead it bore the signs of a more typical college-age kid: dirty dishes in the sink, mail and magazines heaped on various surfaces, a lamp askew, a rug corner flipped up. Or was it more than that? Was this typical post-adolescent slovenliness, or the incipient signs of depression? For example, a plant that my mom had given him had fallen from a window ledge and broken on the floor, but he'd made no effort to sweep up the dirt. And the teakettle he had been so excited about last time I saw him was on the floor next to the couch, knocked over on its side.

I looked up at Raph again and saw suspicion in his eyes. I think the way I was looking around his apartment was making him nervous. "Look," he said, "do you need anything? Because I was just . . ." He trailed off, like he was hoping I would take the hint, but with Chloe in the back of my mind, I pushed forward.

"You were just what?" I said.

"Huh?" he tried, stalling for time. "I was busy. This isn't the best time, Paige, but maybe—"

"Busy with what?" Raph just stared at me. "You're not taking classes, you don't have a job, you don't seem to have any friends other than my mom and me. What exactly are you doing tonight that can't be interrupted?"

Raph swallowed. "I thought I told you," he said. "When someone—"

"When someone changes the subject, when someone makes it clear that they don't want to talk about something, you let it drop, right? Well, I'm not letting it drop this time. I'm sorry, Raph, but I need answers. Logan's been to the hospital twice now. The electronics in the house are going haywire. Total strangers are terrified of the place. This isn't a joke anymore, and it's not something you can just keep to yourself, because you're not the only one affected."

Raph sat down at the counter. "I didn't realize it had gotten that bad."

"You know something," I said. "Tell me what's going on. Tell me what you know."

"How much have you figured out?"

He was deflecting, of course, and I felt a flare of rage at him for continuing to be so evasive when he knew what we were facing. He was as bad as Dr. Clyde, in his way. But I took a deep breath and calmed myself. At least he was acknowledging that there was something to know. This was progress, and if he was willing to go this far, I might get him to go further.

"I know you saw Dr. Clyde," I began, wondering what danger there might be in bluffing. "I know she thinks you're dangerous. And I know . . ."

"What?"

His direct question was making me all too aware of how little I did know. "Something about that pamphlet! That cult. Pronoica. It's tied in with all this somehow."

"Anything else?"

I shook my head, relieved that none of what I said was so off base it would close him off. He scrubbed a hand roughly through his hair.

"I did see Dr. Clyde. I was her patient for almost a year."

"What happened? She said you were cured?"

Raph laughed dryly. "You have a lot to learn about shrinks. No. I stopped going. Maybe I believed I was cured, or maybe I just wanted to be. No, that's not it. I believed I was sick, and that was all I needed to know. That solved all my problems."

"You're doing it again. Talking in riddles."

"Risk you take when you ask people stuff they don't want to tell you."

"It's the morgue, isn't it? You told us it wasn't haunted to throw us off the track, but there's something going on that has to do with—"

"The morgue isn't haunted. It has nothing to do with the morgue."

I sat down across from him. "Why don't you just start at the beginning? Why did you leave school?"

Raph shook his head. "That wasn't the beginning. Not by a long ways. You're asking the wrong questions, Paige."

I flailed about, helplessly. "Fine, then. Start with the boxes. What was in those boxes? Why did you have them here in your apartment?"

"Getting warmer."

"Your professor," I said as a memory from one of our earlier conversations surfaced. "You were working on a project with him . . ."

Raph winced as if he had been slapped. He closed his eyes and didn't open them for a long moment. "Hot yet?" I said. Raph opened his eyes and took a slow, unsteady breath. And indeed, he seemed to be sweating, though the room was as chilly as it had been earlier.

He checked his phone for the time. "Why don't I just show you?" he said. I looked around the apartment, wondering what he had that he could show me, but he shook his head. "Not here." He opened his front door and strode out into the chill night. I followed him.

We walked for blocks, heading toward downtown, but I still had no real idea where we going, just a pit of nervousness in my stomach. As we walked along quiet, treelined residential streets, the cottonwood fluff drifted down on us like a scene from a demented snow globe, and I was struck by the eerie sense that even the seasons had gotten out of joint. None of it made any sense. If my problem was in the house, what solution were we going to find anywhere else? But Raph was so touchy, I was afraid to harass him with more questions than I already had, afraid he would change his mind and head back, or do something even stranger.

Soon we were on the university campus. I had been there a few times to visit Mom in her office, or to see an exhibit at the student art center, but never at night. The dorms and fraternities were brightly lit, and sounds of laughter and camaraderie echoed from them, but we kept walking toward the main quad, which was surrounded by classroom buildings, and was silent and still this time of night. But Raph strode purposefully up the empty paths toward a hulking, modern building, which I realized was the library. There were lights on inside, but otherwise very little sign of life. I read the hours off the sign on the door, then checked my watch. "They're only open another 20 minutes," I said.

"Yes," said Raph, and he opened the door. He gave only the briefest of glances toward the reception desk before moving swiftly toward the stairs and, taking them two at a time so that I panted to keep up, led me up to the fourth floor of the building, then through a maze of library stacks, administrative offices, and storage rooms until we at last reached our apparent destination. The room was filled with boxes, and after a moment's confusion, I realized that they were the same boxes that had been in Raph's apartment not too long ago.

"So this is where they went," I marveled.

"This will tell you most of the story."

The boxes were stacked floor to ceiling, and what labels there were were written in a code that was impenetrable to me. "Where do I begin?"

Raph scanned the room, obviously having something in mind. Then he picked a box from one of the precarious towers, carefully slid it apart from the others, and opened it. "Here," he said, thrusting a slim booklet into my hands, then going back to rifling in the box. I flipped it open and read the title page. *Your Spirit Power: with 20 lessons in how to find it and use it*, it read. I opened it and skimmed through the text.

"What the hell is this stuff?" I said.

"This is our project," said Raph. "This is Pronoica."

The existence of the invisible power in every one of us is fast becoming common knowledge. This omnipresent spirit is the infinite source of all our needs. The invisible spirit of the God-Law lives in you every moment of the day, and is ever waiting for you to recognize that invisible though powerful presence. Please follow me very closely in these studies, for they are pregnant with Spiritual Power.

FRIDAY, JUNE 12, 11:15 A.M.

As Raph's long, pale, nervous fingers sorted efficiently through the various documents in this and a few other boxes, he continued with his story, explaining how he had first come to work with his professor on the Pronoica project.

"I was a sophomore," he said, "and I wasn't even in his department. But I had heard things—that Montague Verano was a genius, that he was far too good for a school like this. Studied in England, and came here for . . . obscure reasons. I was intrigued."

"And?"

"He was everything I'd been promised and more." Raph smiled a private smile. "I was out of my element. I sat in the back of the class and didn't say much. There were other students—seniors, history majors, even a couple of grad students auditing for fun—who were better than me, who stood out in class, who vied with each other for the chance to have even a brief conversation with the man. That was fine with me. I was happy to fly under the radar. I did all the readings, took notes, listened to what everyone else had to say, and felt lucky just to be there, even if no one noticed me."

"But Verano did notice you."

"He . . . took an interest. Called me in after the first paper, and said my work was outstanding. Well beyond his expectations. I was . . . surprised. Flattered. Then he asked me if I wanted to help him with a project he was working on. He said he got the sense that I could keep a secret. I told him I understood."

"Pronoica?"

Raph nodded. "This wasn't an ordinary history book Verano was writing," he went on. "He had an idea—an obsession, you might call it—that Pronoica might be real. Everyone who had looked into it so far had dismissed it just the way you did: as a cult with a charlatan for a leader, who was only trading on people's hopes and dreams to make himself a little cash. But Verano . . . he was convinced there was more to it than that. That maybe even Williamson himself hadn't known what it was, the power he had stumbled into."

"But why did it need to be secret?"

Raph glanced up at me, his eyebrows arched. "You kidding? It would have been career suicide if he'd told anyone what he was working on. This is academia, not some cable TV ghost-hunting show. He had to wait until he had the proof, the evidence he needed to convince the whole world, or they'd write him off as a kook and a crackpot."

"But what was he looking for? What kind of paranormal evidence could you hope to find in some dusty old box?"

"Well . . . ," said Raph, "that was a problem. We had no idea what we were looking for. I kept asking him the same question, but he'd only repeat that historical research doesn't work that way. You can't go in with something specific in mind, or else you'll miss all the other details that are staring you right in the face. You have to be open to anything and everything."

"So you never found anything, then?"

Raph put the papers he had in his hand down carefully. "Not exactly. Or in any case, nothing I could be sure of. A lot of what's in these boxes are testimonials: messages that Williamson's fans and acolytes sent him over the years, explaining how Pronoica had worked for them."

"So it *did* work."

Raph shrugged. "According to some old lady in Texas, sure." He picked a yellowed sheet of notebook paper from a file folder in one of the boxes. "Dear Doctor Williamson," he read, "Thank you again and again for sharing the teachings of Pronoica. Your lessons have truly been a blessing to me. I was going to lose my home, but on that day I discovered one of your pamphlets and learned of the Spiritual Power I contain within myself. The following morning I learned that a recently deceased aunt had left me exactly the amount I needed to release my debts."

"Lucky lady," I said.

"Not-so-lucky aunt," Raph observed. "Anyway, yeah, there was lots of evidence. Williamson's whole career was devoted to collecting evidence of how well his system worked, so he could turn around and pitch it to more people, and get them to subscribe too. But who is it going to convince other than desperate old ladies?"

"It convinced Professor Verano."

Dear Doctor Williamson,

Thank you again and again for sharing the teachings of Pronoica. Your lessons have truly been a blessing to me. I was going to lose my home, but on that day I discovered one of your pamphlets and learned of the Spiritual Power I contain within myself. The following morning I learned that a recently deceased aunt had left me exactly the amount I needed to release my debts.

"Not the testimonials—something else. To this day, I'm not sure if it even makes any sense. But when I got frustrated, he told me to change my tactic. He said there was more to all these letters and documents than what people were saying—we had to be alert to what they *weren't* saying. Things glimpsed out of the corner of the eye, that might lead us to what was really going on. That's what led me to the Pronoica Clinic."

"The clinic? What's that?"

Raph gave a wry smile. "Once again, no one knows. In all these hundreds, maybe thousands, of documents, I only ever found one reference to the Pronoica Clinic. But it stuck with me, because it was different from the other stuff. Something physical. Something present. Not a pamphlet sent through the mail, but a real place, in this very town."

Raph flipped through the files once more, this time his fingers stopping at something and tugging it up from the box. He handed it to me.

"PRONOICA CLINIC," it read. Then, "A private institution devoted to the ethical and scientific practice of Medicine and Surgery as an adjunct to the healing power of the Spirit of God. Located at Moscow, Idaho." Underneath it was a photograph of a squat Victorian mansion with a turret and a wraparound porch.

"The house," I said softly. I looked up to meet his eyes. "The clinic—it was in our house. So that's why . . ." I shook my head. "But it doesn't make sense. All these pamphlets, all the testimonials. This was no devil-worshipping cult. Williamson believed in the same kind of stuff my mom does: positive energy and being the good you want to see in the universe. That kind of junk. So why does the house seem so . . . angry?"

PRONOICA CLINIC

A private institution devoted to the ethical and scientific practice of Medicine and Surgery as an adjunct to the healing power of the Spirit of God. Located at Moscow, Idaho.

"Maybe the pamphlets and the testimonials don't tell the whole story."

"What are you saying?" I asked. "That Pronoica has some kind of dark side? That Williamson and his followers were conjuring demons in their spare time?" I meant it as a joke, but something about the way Raph shrugged made me uneasy.

"Not on purpose, maybe," he said. "But what if all that spiritual power they were playing with stirred up something they didn't know how to control?"

"In the house, you mean. The clinic. You think something happened there that they weren't expecting," I guessed. "Something Williamson tried to cover up. Is that why the place is messing with us now?"

"I don't know," he said, "but think about it. It's one thing to send people hopeful messages through the mail, but if he was telling people to travel here from all over the country—sick and injured people—so that he could heal them through some mixture of faith and pseudoscience . . ."

"Yeah, I see it now. Something could have gone seriously wrong."

"Whatever it was, he did a good job hushing it up. No mention of it anywhere. Not in his documents, not in the local papers, or any public record."

"So what about Verano? What did he think of it?"

Raph didn't answer.

"You did tell him, right?"

Raph got to his feet and started rifling through another box, not meeting my eye.

"Right, I get it," I said. "You're changing the subject. We only ever get to talk about the stuff you want to talk about."

Just then, the door opened behind me, and I whirled around to see who it was. It was a young woman, the one I had seen down at the circulation desk when we came in.

"Just letting you know that the library is closing. You need to start heading out now, or . . ." She stopped, in the middle of a thought. "Raph?" she said. "What are you doing here?"

"It's fine, I—don't worry, Lizzie. I just wanted to check something, is all. We'll be going right now, you don't have to—"

"You're not supposed to be here. They told me to call security if I ever saw you, I could get in a lot of trouble, if—"

Raph took a deep breath. "You're not going to get into any trouble because you're not going to tell anyone. My friend and I were just leaving. We're going straight home. We don't want any trouble, and neither do you. Right?"

Lizzie still stood in the doorway, not speaking, clearly deliberating. "Lizzie," said Raph again, and this time his voice was not nervous or hard-edged, as it so frequently was, but soft and kind . . . and even—could it be?—a little flirtatious. He gave her a winning smile that transformed his whole face from a dark and brooding creature weighed down by who knew what troubles to a charming and stunningly handsome college boy, irresistible in his every movement. He leaned almost imperceptibly closer to her. "You know there's nothing to be afraid of. It's only me."

I could see the war going on behind Lizzie's eyes—a strange mixture of apprehension and desire. At last she stepped away from the door. "Seriously, go straight home. You shouldn't be here, and I don't want to get into trouble."

The smile dropped suddenly from his face, but he grabbed

my hand and tugged me to the door. "Come on, Paige. We've seen what we needed to see."

Raph speed-walked all the way home, and I could barely keep up with him, let alone assault him with all the questions that were swirling around in my head. When we got back to the house, I tried to follow him into his apartment, but he made it clear there would be no more discussion tonight. "Your mother will wonder where you are," he said darkly, and he closed the door in my face.

MONDAY, JUNE 15, 10:12 A.M.

I woke up this morning into what is essentially a hellscape. The air is heavy and dark and smells wonderful, and a scary blood-orange ball reigns over it all.

Logan came inside while I was eating breakfast and said, did you see the moon this morning? It was bright red.

I said, that wasn't the moon, you dummy, it was the sun, but he was pretty sure, and we wound up looking up sunrise and moonset timetables. (I was right.)

I know this is because of the fires burning over in Washington. It's a weird day when you can't tell the difference between the sun and the moon.

TUESDAY, JUNE 16, 12:16 A.M.

After three days of Raph avoiding me, I finally made Chloe come over after school to help me corner him. We stood together on his doorstep while I knocked, but no one came to the door.

"Now what?" I said.

Chloe put her ear to the door. "I can hear movement."

"Doesn't do us much good if he's ignoring us."

"Let's make ourselves harder to ignore, then." I stared at her and she rolled her eyes. "We know he doesn't lock his door, remember?"

Raph was at least dressed this time, but he surprised me by not demanding immediately that we leave. He looked almost as though he had been expecting this visit. As if he viewed it as unpleasant but inevitable.

"Ladies," he said, but I wasn't interested in playing his games this time.

"Why aren't you allowed on campus?" I asked.

"I don't think that's any of your business."

"You brought me there, Raph. You made me an accomplice to your violating . . . what, a restraining order? I don't even know, but you dragged me into it, and now it is my business. So why don't you tell me what exactly is going on."

"It's nothing," he said forcefully. "I'm telling you, it's not what you're thinking. It's nothing to do with . . . It was a misunderstanding, that's all."

"The kind of misunderstanding that makes someone call the police?" said Chloe.

Raph glared at her. "Last semester I—" He stopped himself and took a deep breath. "I was behaving erratically," he went on. "Or so I'm told. People were concerned. For my safety, and for the safety of . . . others. But I'm not supposed to . . . It was part of the agreement, I swore I wouldn't . . ." Raph thrust a hand into his hair and tugged, as if using the pain to balance out some inner turmoil. He seemed to be speaking mostly to himself now. "He said it could do a lot of damage, if anyone . . . it would ruin everything. And anyway, I brought it on myself. Things had been going so well. We were getting so close. And all I wanted was . . . of course he had warned me, but I didn't see . . . it all seemed harmless . . . until it wasn't."

Chloe and I watched him in silence for a minute. He seemed close to giving us the answers we were looking for, and I didn't want to spook him. "Who warned you?" I said gently. "About what?"

Raph looked up and seemed almost surprised that we were

still there. Then he seemed to come to some realization. "You want to know about Pronoica," he said, as if that hadn't been obvious all along. "I can tell you about that. As long as I . . ." He stood up and paced a little, gathering his thoughts. "Yes," he said at last, sounding much more normal. "All right. You know already about Verano's obsession. He wanted to know if Williamson had been on to anything, if any of it was real. He had me combing through those documents, endless documents, hours and hours each day until my eyes ached."

"Right," I said. "So?"

"So, I got sick of it. And I thought—I knew there was a simpler way."

I waited for him to continue. "Simpler?" I prompted when he didn't.

"It's obvious, isn't it? I decided to try it. Williamson's methods."

"The stuff from the mailings? You mean the kooky meditation exercises he gave the little old ladies?"

Raph shrugged lightly.

"Did anything . . . happen?"

"Not much at first. Just a sense of peace, an aura of well-being. Nice enough, but you can get that much at any yoga studio these days. But after a week or so, it really kicked in."

I exchanged a look with Chloe.

"Material blessings," he said. "'The Living Spirit can bring to you perfect abundance. The World may be yours, and everything in it.' This is the key to Pronoica. Williamson didn't just promise his followers spiritual bliss, or a ticket to eternal salvation. He promised them cash."

"And you . . . that *worked*?"

Raph grinned. "Found twenty bucks in my pocket the

first day. A week later, got a job offer for the summer. I even won a couple hundred dollars off a lotto ticket. But it wasn't just that . . . it was weirder stuff too. More personal. I'd get a burger at Zips, and when I got home, there'd be two in the bag. Kept finding songs on my hard drive that I couldn't remember downloading. I'd do laundry and wind up with twice as many socks as I'd started with. I had never been very lucky before, but now I felt . . . more than lucky. I felt blessed.

"Still, nothing you'd want to contact the local news over. It wasn't proof exactly, but it was exciting." He began moving again. "I was a convert, you could say, just like Williamson's followers had been. I wanted to share my good fortune with the world. Or at least a few friends." He cast a sharp look at Chloe. "Yes, I did have friends. Then." He sat down on a stool for a moment before popping up again. "None of them took it too seriously, and it became kind of a joke around the department. People teased me about it, and others got concerned, and the whole thing wound up getting back to Verano.

"He was furious. He said it was dangerous to undertake an experiment like this when we had so little information. He called me foolish, said I had lost my sense of scholarly remove. And I . . . I . . . well, never mind about that." Raph's shoulders slumped. "Around that time I was advised to take some time off, to collect myself. That's when I moved in here. And started seeing Dr. Clyde."

"Did you tell her about all this?"

"About Pronoica? Some. I tried to. But she had other things she was more interested in dissecting."

I nodded grimly. "I know that story. Somehow you always wind up talking about what she wants to talk about."

241

"And she was convinced it was all in my head. I can't really blame her—in all honesty, I wasn't exactly acting like a man in possession of all his faculties. There were . . . strikes against me in that department already. It was a relief, actually," he said. "Turns out I was more comfortable playing the delusional nutcase than the only living prophet of a kook religion that died out half a century ago. And I couldn't deny that her approach worked. I took her pills, I did her visualization exercises, and everyone agreed I was doing much better."

"I don't understand, though," I said. "This still doesn't explain why the house started acting up the minute my family moved in."

"I know," said Raph. "People have been calling this place haunted for years, but it was always some old story remembered off a friend of a friend of a friend. Then when I started working on the place, I'd get . . . bad feelings. Dreams. A sense that I wasn't completely alone. But nothing like what's been happening recently." He shook his head. "Something must have changed."

TUESDAY, JUNE 16, 3:58 A.M.

I don't know what possessed me to go to sleep in this house after that conversation with Raph. For some idiotic reason I was feeling better about the whole thing—like we were closing in on the reasons for everything that has gone on here. But having the reasons isn't the same as making everything go away! Why did I think it was? I didn't think it, really. Not consciously. But on some level I must have believed it, because after our talk Chloe went home and I went upstairs and I typed everything that had happened into my journal, and it all seemed . . . so *exciting*. Like I was finally on the trail of something real. Finally getting some answers. And I went to bed feeling calm and contented, like we had made real progress.

Then I woke up.

It was still dark out. Normally at this point I would look

at the clock and then turn over and try to get back to sleep, or sometimes listen closely to see if I could figure out what Logan might be doing. But this time I didn't have to listen. Logan was sitting on the edge of my bed. Watching me.

When I saw him, my adrenaline spiked so bad I nearly jumped out of bed. Even though this wasn't the first time, there was something deeply unsettling about his presence there. He wasn't trying to wake me up to tell me something, or just sitting with me for company, or anything even vaguely normal like that. He was just . . . staring at me. When he saw that I was awake, saw me looking at him, he smiled.

"Logan?" I said cautiously. "Are you okay?" But the look on his face made it plenty clear that he was not.

He smiled even bigger. "Hey, Paige," he said, and the weird thing was, his voice was totally normal. I don't know why that's weird. That's the opposite of weird, right? But I was expecting him to sound ethereal or strange in some way, or, if he were a normal kid waking his sister in the middle of the night, he might sound scared or embarrassed or something. But his tone . . . he was talking to me as if he had just found me in the kitchen in the middle of the day. As if there were nothing remotely weird about any of it. And that was what creeped me out.

He must have seen the expression on my face because he immediately said, "Don't worry, Paige. I was getting rid of them for you."

Um . . . what?

"The spiders," he said. "I know you don't like them, so I just sit here and pick them off you."

I didn't say anything. I couldn't say anything. I just stared at him in wide-eyed horror.

"I think I'm beginning to understand why you don't like them," he went on. "I've been studying them. Did you know that they pulsate when they eat things alive? All eight legs, pulsing, like a heart that only knows how to eat things. Creepy, right? But don't worry, they don't do it all night long. They usually come out around 3 in the morning, or a little after. And by 4:30 they're gone. But if I don't stop by between 3 and 4, it gets real bad. One night I was doing something else, and didn't make it here until 3:30. And when I got here, I couldn't even see your face. It was just a solid mass of swarming black spiders. Oh, don't be afraid, Paige. They haven't hurt you yet. And they don't usually even wake you up. I promise, they are perfectly harmless."

It's a good thing I was frozen to the bed, or else I might well have clawed all the flesh from my face.

Then Logan put out a hand toward my hairline, just above my ear. "Oh!" he said. "There's one. Don't move." And he picked something off my face and held it up in front of my eyes. He held it by one leg, but the other seven danced before my eyes in a way that turned my stomach. "I can hear the birds now," he said. "It's almost 4 now, so the spiders will be pretty much done. I'm going to get back to my letter."

And he got up and left the room.

Holy Christ, what do I do? What the fuck, what the fuck. Why are there spiders? Why is Logan like this? I can't be alone with him. And Mom isn't even home tonight. She's sleeping over at Arthur's. I can't be alone with him. What do I do?

TUESDAY, JUNE 16, 4:10 A.M.

Mom's not answering my texts, so I tried Raph. I need to be around someone sane or . . . sane-ish. I guess most people would say (have said) that Raph isn't the best choice, but he's the only person who gets it. The only person I can deal with seeing right now. Oh, he just texted back, thank God.

He wrote:

> It's the middle of the night. What's going on?

What does he think is going on? Okay, texted him:

> I'm scared, I can't be alone with him. Something awful . . .

I really can't bring myself to describe that whole scene over text. Ugh God, what is he doing? Why isn't he texting back? Okay, he just texted back.

> K. The door's open.

TUESDAY, JUNE 16, 4:25 A.M.

I think I am safe now. Posting from my phone, in Raph's apartment. He's gone back to bed, and I'm going to try to get some rest on his couch. Phone's being weird, though. I've gotten six texts in the past half hour and none of them make any sense. I don't know if it's Mom trying to contact me or . . . I don't know.

I don't like leaving Logan alone in the house, but . . . honestly, I don't want to be around him right now.

TUESDAY, JUNE 16, 7:54 A.M.

I don't fully understand what happened last night. I don't even really remember it. The best I can do is write it out to try to piece this back together.

I crept down the stairs after Raph's last text, doing my best to avoid Logan. The last thing I needed was him asking me where I was going, or realizing he was alone in the house. And I made it out the front door and then down to Raph's apartment, where the door was unlocked as usual. The whole place was dark, of course, except for some thin moonlight coming in from those small windows. I picked my way through the shadows toward Raph's bedroom, at the back of the apartment. I'd never been in there before. It was darker even than the other rooms, and I could barely make out the outline of Raph's dark curls against the white of his pillow.

"Raph," I whispered hoarsely. No answer. "Raph," I said again, in something closer to a normal voice.

"What?" he said. "Oh, right, Paige." He sat up in bed. "I'm sorry, I drifted off again." He rubbed a hand over his face and scraped it through his hair. "Is this real? I was dreaming, and then—"

"It's not a dream." If only!

Raph, just like on the night I met him, was shirtless. He was under covers, but I figured that if experience was any indication, he was probably wearing nothing but underwear. I felt suddenly self-conscious about being in my goofy pajamas, but . . . God, the brain is a weird organ. I can't believe I was even thinking about stuff like that, given what had just happened. But at least it was distracting me a little from the horror.

"What's going on?" Raph said, jolting me out of my nervous silence. I gave him a recap, with as much detail as I could bear. For a minute or so, he didn't say anything.

"Raph," I said.

"What do you want me to do?"

"I don't know. Nothing, I know there's nothing . . . I just . . . I can't go back up there. I can't be alone. Can I . . . stay here with you?"

Raph closed his eyes. "I don't know if that's a good idea."

"I know," I said. "It's dangerous, you're dangerous. So you keep telling me. But at least down here my face isn't covered in spiders."

Raph opened his eyes again, and I saw resignation and sympathy in them. "Okay," he said. "You can crash on the couch until morning."

I thanked him and groped my way through the dark back to his couch. I tried to sleep for a couple minutes, but I was way too jumpy, so eventually I took out my phone, just to distract myself. Even so, though, I kept feeling—or *thinking* I felt—tiny legs tickling my skin. I shook my limbs and smacked at the strange sensations until my skin was red and raw, but I never saw anything.

Eventually I couldn't bear it anymore and I snuck back toward Raph's room. He was asleep again, stretched out in a moonbeam, his face peaceful, his pale skin almost glowing. Instantly I felt calmer. No matter how many warnings people gave me, including Raph himself, I just couldn't see him as dangerous. In the madness I now faced every day, he felt like an island of sanity.

There wasn't anyplace else in the room to sit, so I eased myself gently onto the edge of the bed, not wanting to disturb him. Idly I wondered about his history, the stuff he didn't want to tell us. About what had gone wrong that had resulted in him getting kicked off campus. A failed romance, presumably. Gazing down on his elegant sleeping form, it was hard to picture anyone rejecting him. What kind of person could resist this gorgeous creature, as broken and tortured as he might be?

Eventually I started to get stiff in my position, so I carefully shifted and scooched in a bit to sit next to him in the bed, my back leaning against the headboard.

I was convinced there was no way I would be able to sleep that night, but the next thing I remember, my eyelids shot open as if I'd just received a shot of adrenaline.

I didn't remember where I was, or maybe even who I was.

Everything felt strange and wrong, and my whole body was trembling, my muscles spasming. I sat straight up in the bed, and after a moment felt my senses returning to me. I'm in Raph's bedroom. There is a weird, thick feeling in my throat, as if I swallowed a penny or something. My pajamas are all twisted up, and also sticking to me because I'm coated in a slick film of sweat. The bedclothes are tangled around me as if someone has been thrashing wildly in the bed, and they are also damp, presumably with sweat. I am alone in the bed, my breathing shallow and labored, my pulse erratic.

I took a few deep, slow breaths, like my mom taught me for dealing with exam stress and stuff—in through my nose, one two three, out through my mouth, one two three—and gradually started to feel like myself again. It was at this point that I realized I could hear voices. A voice. Raph's voice. Coming from the kitchen.

I got out of bed and moved quietly toward his voice. From the doorway I could see him facing away from me, leaning over the kitchen sink. He had slipped on a pair of jeans and he was talking on his phone, but there was something weird about his voice, like it was slightly muffled.

"I'm sorry," he was saying. "I know. I know, but this is different." His voice was trembling and his words seemed to come with difficulty. "You have to come, please . . . It isn't about that! I swear." Raph paused to listen, and hung his head at whatever he was hearing. "I know. And I promise I wouldn't call if it weren't—" [pause] "I understand all that, and look, in six months I haven't talked to you once, I haven't contacted you, I haven't—I've abided by the—but this is different, it's not just about me." [pause] "Monty, listen to what I'm saying!

I don't care. You started this, you can't just walk away when you feel like it." [pause] "I told you." [pause] "You promise?" [pause] "Yeah, okay, I know, just . . . come quickly."

Raph hung up the phone and turned around. He startled a little when he saw me. My mouth was already moving to ask, "Who's Monty?" but the words were replaced by a different question when I saw his face. I realized now why his voice sounded weird: he had a dish towel pressed up against his mouth. "What happened?" I said. "Are you okay?"

Raph dropped his hand with the dish towel to his side, revealing a large, messy gash in his lip, which looked like it had only recently stopped gushing and started to seal itself. As he stood up straighter in the sunlight, I saw something else: there were tiny reddish bruises, maybe the size of a nickel, all over his chest, his throat, and a few on his wrists. I gasped and rushed to his side. I was just trying to help. I wanted to examine his injuries, clean them, and see if they needed a doctor's attention. But Raph moved away from me. In fact, he was . . . cowering, shrinking away from me, backing himself up against the refrigerator, his eyes big with fear.

Growing desperate, I kept asking what happened, if he was okay, should I call a doctor, but he wouldn't answer. Then something caught my eye from the counter: a smear of bright color reflected at me in the chrome side of the toaster. It was me. My face and chest, red with blood.

I touched my face, not believing what I saw, but my fingers came away sticky with the stuff. "Raph . . . ," I said uncertainly. "What happened to us?"

Raph squeezed his eyes shut. "Leave me alone," he whispered. "Please, get away from me."

I ran all the way to our upstairs bathroom and set about cleaning the blood from my skin. The strange thing is, though I checked my whole face and neck and the inside of my mouth, I couldn't find a cut.

I don't think it was my blood.

TUESDAY, JUNE 16, 8:13 A.M.

I'm panicking. I texted Mom so many times last night, but now I don't want to see her. Don't want to try to explain the inexplicable. Where would I even begin? But she just got home. She's banging on my bedroom door, asking if I am okay. She sounds so scared. Of course she is scared, after the crazy texts I sent.

Okay, if I wait any longer, she's going to break down the door. I better face her.

TUESDAY, JUNE 16, 11:23 A.M.

Mom gave me a big hug when I opened the door and checked me over. Good thing I'd cleaned up all the blood and changed my clothes, or she would have really freaked. But before I got a chance to explain anything, the doorbell rang.

Mom looked at her watch. "Who could that be?" I had an idea, but I kept silent.

We both headed downstairs, and as we passed the kitchen, I noticed Logan sitting at the table and eating a bowl of cereal, as if this were the most ordinary Tuesday morning in the world. "Morning," he said, his mouth half-full. I stared at him, boggled at the difference between my kid brother now and whatever he was last night. "Hey," I said, more out of habit than anything else, and I followed Mom to the door.

The man standing there looked strangely out of place in this sleepy Idaho town. I hadn't seen a man in such a finely cut suit since Dad took me to one of his movie premieres. He was small and slight, probably in his late 40s, but with a dramatic shock of prematurely snow-white hair. His eyes were a piercing, icy blue, and he carried a cane with an ornate silver handle.

"Good morning," he said, holding out one hand. "Montague Verano. I'm a professor of history at the university. My apologies for disturbing you at this hour on a fine summer morning, but I've come to search your house."

For a moment, Mom just stared at him in blank surprise. Meanwhile, gears clicked in my brain. Montague Verano—*Monty*. And sure enough, I realized that Raph was standing a few feet behind him, his hands thrust awkwardly into his pockets.

"I'm sorry?" Mom tried at last, taking his hand as almost an afterthought. But Verano was regarding her just as closely, and instead of shaking her hand, he pulled it toward his body.

"You seem quite familiar to me," he said, running his eyes over her face. "Have we met before?"

"Um," she said, caught off guard. "No, we don't—that is, I—I get that a lot."

Verano dropped her hand and made a movement toward her, crowding her against the doorjamb. "Yes," he said with a nod. "You have an old soul?"

"No," said Mom. "I mean, yes, but—no—I was in movies. You've probably seen them."

"I don't watch movies," said Verano. "Which ones?"

"*Some Sacred Summer? Dayton Tuscaloosa? High School High?*"

Verano raised an eyebrow. "Is that the one with the dead skunk in the bathroom?" Mom nodded. "I may have seen it on a plane."

At this point, it looked like Mom was becoming over-whelmed by Verano's forced proximity, and she stepped away from him—a move that he apparently took as an invitation to enter the house. I took some pleasure in the sour look on his face as he was forced to navigate the cloud of flies.

Raph followed just behind him, his shoulders hunched in discomfort at the whole scene, though I guess with Verano here, he was no longer too nervous to enter the house at all.

"These all yours?" said Verano, examining her assortment of dream catchers and ritual candles. Mom nodded. "Quite a nice collection," he observed, which coaxed a smile out of her. "Many of these items could be picked up at any one of the innumerable and interchangeable New Age bookshops that dot this country, but a few of these are rare pieces."

Verano's accent was unplaceable. It sounded British to me at first, maybe by way of Swiss boarding school. Then, as he went on, his vowels became rounded in a much more American way . . . but every few words that hint of clipped, foreign speech would reassert itself for a syllable or two. I couldn't decide if this meant that he had lived all over, or if it was meant to con-vey that impression. He was clearly someone who cared a lot about his image, so I didn't rule that possibility out.

"Thank you," said Mom. "I started collecting after the—"

But Professor Verano didn't appear to be listening. He glanced over his shoulder at Raph. "Find me a trash bag, would you please."

"Wait, what?" said Mom as Verano began pulling her trinkets down from the shelves. "What do you think you're doing?"

"I understand you have a problem with spirits."

"You misunderstand, then. We don't have a problem.

258

Professor . . . Verano, is it? I appreciate your interest, but as I've explained to my daughter many times, it's only human prejudice that makes people afraid of the spirit world. In this household we respect our neighbors, embodied or otherwise. We are not in need of an exorcism."

"Mom!" I exclaimed. "Stop it." Given his rude behavior, I wasn't eager to take Verano's side against my own mother, but I had to admit that his confident manner gave me hope that he might know how to resolve our situation. At the least, he was the first person who seemed willing to take it seriously. "Stop acting like this is all a cute little game," I said to her. "Look what happened to Logan, look at what has happened to all of us. Whatever is in this house does not have our best interests at heart."

Verano unceremoniously dropped a clinking armload of my mom's ritual objects into the bag Raph had found. "Ms. Blanton," he said, "you should heed your daughter. I don't think you fully appreciate the nature of the forces affecting this house, and your family. Your trinkets have done more harm than good here. You have disturbed some very powerful forces, and you are now in a position of considerable danger. Your sage smudging, your altars and dream catchers and crystals and grimoires . . . It all seems quite harmless to you, but it may not seem so benevolent to . . ." He raised his eyes toward the ceiling, almost as if he could see a demon squatting there. "To others," he finished.

Then, with barely a glance more in her direction, Verano proceeded to show himself around the first floor of the house, moving swiftly from room to room, stopping here and there to press his ear to the walls and tap the head of his cane three times.

"What—what are you looking for?" I asked.

"Amelia," he replied in a hushed voice.

"Who's Amelia?" I said, but Verano was in his own world, and showed no inclination to answer. Raph, luckily, was able to fill us in.

"Amelia was Williamson's daughter. She shows up a bunch in Pronoica stuff when she's a baby, but she disappears from the record when she's around 13."

"Exactly!" shouted Verano from the pantry. "An absence. A very significant absence."

"What does that prove, though?" asked Mom. Verano came in through the kitchen and stood very close to her.

"Nothing," he said with a strange smile. "Nothing at all. But it is suggestive, isn't it?"

"Are you thinking that something happened with Amelia at the clinic?" said Raph. "That she saw something, something she shouldn't have, and they needed to shut her up?"

"Yes," said Verano, "yes, I believe . . ." But he stopped himself, and his eyes grew large with some sudden realization. "Ah yes, shut her up. Exactly," he said. "Don't you see, Raphael? She didn't just disappear from the record, she *disappeared*."

"You mean he killed her?"

"Possibly. But no. I think that he . . ." Suddenly he turned toward me. "Do you know of any unaccounted-for spaces in this house? A blocked-up door, or a room that seems too small for its place in the house?"

I glanced at Mom and Logan. "There is a blocked-up door, but it just leads down to Raph's apartment. I don't know any other—"

"The turret," said Logan. "My room is under a turret, but the ceiling is flat. There must be some extra space up there."

260

Verano said nothing, but his face lit up, and he dashed up the stairs, his cane clenched purposelessly in his fist.

We followed him up, but before I even reached the top of the stairs, I heard him emit a sharp cry. I exchanged a look with Mom before running up the remaining steps. "Professor Verano? Are you—"

As he came into view, I saw his face scrunched into a pained expression, one hand rubbing vigorously at his head. "That sound," he said. "How can you bear it?"

"Oh," I said. "You can hear it? It's actually not so bad today. Some days it sounds like—"

"For God's sake, child, how long have you been living with this? A room in your house produces noises like a direct portal to hell, and you . . . what? Put your headphones on?" I didn't have a good answer to this, and he didn't seem to expect one. Instead he gritted his teeth and went into the room, eyeing the ceiling with academic interest.

"Raphael," he said. "In that toolbox of yours, do you happen to have a sledge hammer?"

TUESDAY, JUNE 16, 12:30 P.M.

Raph does not have a sledgehammer, as it turns out, but he figures his crowbar should do the trick.

The others are all eyeing the ceiling nervously, but I look straight at him and nod when he asks if we are ready. Something is up there, I can just feel it. Something that will at last make everything make sense.

He's standing on a chair now. Swinging the crowbar back and forth to get some momentum. He's made his first crack at the ceiling, but it just produced a lot of plaster dust. This is weirdly like playing piñata.

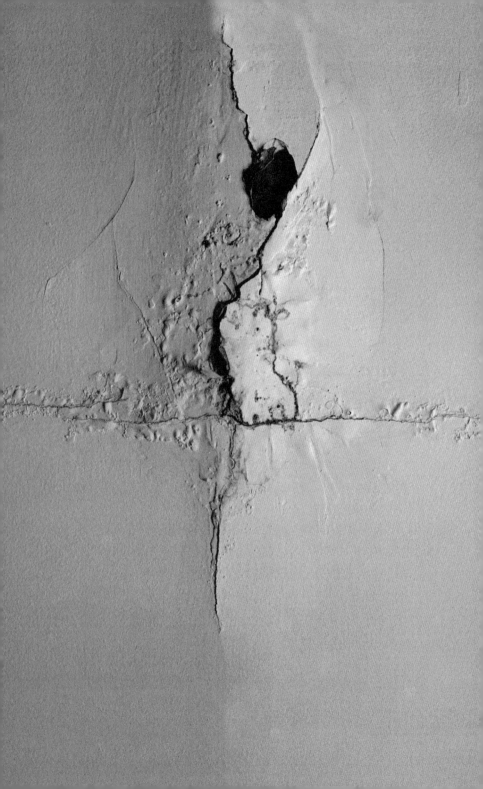

TUESDAY, JUNE 16, 1:37 P.M.

I passed out the minute the spiders started pouring down. That's all I remember. I was staring straight up at the ceiling, we all were, and then black, hairy confetti was raining down. It took a second for me to register, but once I did, I don't think I even had a chance to shriek. I was out for the count.

The next thing I remember, I was coming to on the living room couch. I immediately started spasming, and I think Mom and Logan thought it was a seizure at first, but it was just me trying to get the spiders off. There weren't any spiders by then, though, so I just wound up tearing my clothes to shreds.

I don't know how I'll ever sleep again. Even without being conscious through most of it, just the knowledge that I spent those minutes in a flood of . . . In my hair, in my ears, under my clothes . . . Logan and the others had been quite diligent about removing them all before I woke up, but that just leaves the question . . . where are they now? Because I'm pretty sure they didn't kill them all.

TUESDAY, JUNE 16, 2:00 P.M.

Verano says that wasn't what we were looking for. We have to keep looking. I'm not sure I can, not sure I can take the risk of facing what we might find. Not after that last experience. And yet at this point, how can I not? And what could possibly be worse?

I don't know. In a weird way, I think that experience might have cured me. When I was a kid, I'd shriek and cry and run even at toy spiders. I was so scared. But how can any of that scare me now? Now that I've seen and experienced . . . It's like I dug deep enough into the terror, I came out on the other side. I can't be afraid of spiders anymore. I'm not sure I can be afraid of anything.

TUESDAY, JUNE 16, 2:36 P.M.

After some time to recuperate, we reconvened in Logan's room. The buzzing was even more painful now. I'm not sure why I even still refer to it as "the buzzing," except out of habit, or maybe for continuity's sake. Verano was right: I think I had been repressing it, simply refusing to hear it properly for weeks, out of pure force of will. But his comment had brought it back to the surface, and now that it was there, it was just as he said: shrieking, howling, the mad chattering of a thousand lost souls.

I think the others were finally noticing it too, though no one's expression looked as pained as Verano's. Except mine. Not that I could see myself, but looking at him and seeing the anguish written on his face felt like looking in a mirror.

Mom took a look around the room—swept out now, but still with a handful of spiders creeping around in the corners—and said, "There's nothing here, let's go back downstairs," but Verano ignored her. He was staring up at the giant hole in the ceiling.

"It doesn't make sense," he said. This comment seemed like such an understatement, it hardly required a response. But Verano had something specific in mind. "Is there a third floor to this house?"

"Only the basement, where Raph lives." Mom started to move toward the bedroom door, but Verano didn't. Instead he pulled his phone from the pocket of his coat, and started to enter something into it.

"Phones don't really work in the house," I told him.

He nodded. "So I've heard. But I'm not trying to call anyone." After a moment he tucked his phone back into his pocket. "There's something wrong with this room," he said.

"No shit," muttered Logan. Mom made a disapproving noise but didn't correct him.

"Not just this room, though," said Verano. "This whole floor. It's too short."

"What?"

"I knew there was something off about it as soon as we came up the stairs. This building is from the Victorian era. You don't have to be an art historian to know that in a grand house like this, architects of the time preferred very high ceilings. This building would have been no exception. In its first incarnation it had a ballroom and a grand receiving room. Those certainly would have been quite high. But when we were in your living room . . . the ceilings there are barely eight feet. I wondered if, during some remodel, the extra space had been shifted to the second floor. But no—the ceilings here are quite low as well. So where did the extra space go?"

We all looked up. Through the hole Raph had created, it was more than obvious that there was nothing between us and the roof other than a couple of layers of beams and insulation. Verano furrowed his brow, puzzled, but wheels were turning in my head.

"The windows," I said. Everyone turned. "Chloe mentioned it ages ago, but I never gave it much thought. There are windows . . . you can see them from the outside. And they don't correspond with anything on the inside." Verano stared at me, comprehension dawning.

"It's below us. Between the floors."

We considered ripping up the floorboards, but Mom had the idea that it would be easier, safer, and cause less permanent damage if we approached from the side, via the stairwell. It made sense, after all, that if we were trying to find a hidden floor between the known levels, the staircase would be the best way in.

Verano and Raph spent some time tapping at the walls and fiddling with tools, listening for hollow spaces and trying to avoid load-bearing beams. Eventually they found the spot they wanted, and Raph wielded the crowbar again. I prepared myself for another tidal wave of spiders, or God only knew what other monstrosity, but this time we were greeted only by a handful of lazily swooping flies and a cloud of plaster.

When the dust cleared, Verano put his head through the hole. "It's empty," he said, and stepped aside so the rest of us

could look. It was true. The space was much bigger than an ordinary crawl space—tall enough for an adult man to stand up straight inside. Light shone in from the windows Chloe had noticed, suggesting that this had once been a real part of the house. Rooms where people lived, not just insulation. But all we could see were beams and plaster and dust, plus a handful of tools left over from the last remodel, presumably. Except . . .

"There's a door," I said. "Look, at the opposite end. That's not just the exterior wall. There's a door there."

The others peered in and confirmed what I had seen, and moments later we were smashing through the wall to create a hole big enough for us each to climb through. I was surprised to note that there weren't any spiders in this part of the house—there didn't seem to be much sign of any living thing, in fact. Once through, we picked our way carefully across the unfinished floor toward the door. It wouldn't budge.

"It's locked," said Raph. "I could probably bust through it with the crowbar, though."

"That won't be necessary," said Verano. "This door was locked from the outside. This lock wasn't meant to keep people out—it was meant to keep someone in."

"To shut her up," I said.

Verano ran his flashlight over the door until his eye caught on a latch. Sure enough, it was a simple deadbolt. One twist of the knob, and the door swung open, releasing a blast of air so cold it made me catch my breath, followed by a swarm of fat, black flies whose wings beat slowly and solidly against my skin.

I wasn't the only one who screamed in alarm, but before long they had dissipated (or, more likely, gone to join their revolting brethren), and we were able to move into the room.

It was completely dark inside except for a couple of hairlines of bright light coming from the far side. "That must be one of the missing windows," said Verano, his breath visible even though it was a warm summer day outside. "Boarded up." *To keep anyone from seeing her*, he didn't say, but we were all thinking it.

Raph had a couple of flashlights in his toolbox, so we shone those around a bit. The room was sparsely furnished: a chair and desk with a washbasin, and a metal cot in the corner. What was stranger were the weird squishy shapes on the wall. I pressed on them. It was like a big couch cushion or something had been nailed there.

"It's padded," said Mom. "A padded cell." The term conjured images in my head of people wrapped in straitjackets, throwing themselves at every surface uncontrollably.

"You mean like for crazy people?"

"Perhaps," said Verano. "It would make sense. If she was—"

"No," said Logan. He hadn't spoken in so long, I had sort of forgotten he was there. Suddenly I felt weird about him being there. He's just a kid. Should he be seeing all this stuff, when we didn't even know exactly what we might see? On the other hand, he had lived through the worst of what the house had to offer. Maybe he was entitled to see where it all came from.

"Not crazy," said Logan softly. "Epileptic."

"How do you . . . ," I began, but one look at Logan's face told me how he had guessed. Of course. The doctors couldn't find the cause of Logan's seizures, because they didn't come from his brain.

They came from Amelia. And if Amelia had seizures, like Logan . . . without modern medicine, they wouldn't have been

273

able to do much for her, except stick her in a padded room and hope she didn't hurt herself too much.

"But then why lock her in?" I said. "It doesn't make sense. It's medieval. So what if she had epilepsy? Why would they want to lock her away from the world for years?"

"He would need to hide anything that seemed potentially negative," said Verano. "He was the prophet of a religion that demanded that only good things happen to him. If anyone were to find out that he'd had any kind of bad luck, the entire religion would start to look like a sham. So he had to hide her away."

I couldn't repress a shiver, though whether it was because of the frigid air that had been locked in this room for almost a century, or because of Verano's comments, I couldn't say. Before I could dwell on the question, Mom pointed out something the rest of us hadn't noticed: an old trunk in the corner of the room. In a minute or two Raph had the lock broken and the top pried open. "Holy shit," he said as he tipped open the top. The flashlight beams danced over the contents of the chest.

They were letters.

"Jackpot," said Raph.

"What do you mean?" I asked.

"We always suspected," said Verano, "that there were other letters, outside the official record . . . letters Williamson either destroyed or hid away."

"And you think . . ."

Verano let out a low whistle. "The missing letters."

For I don't even know how long, we all crouched around Raph, hunched to share the light of two flashlights, trying to read as much as we could of the letters. It was a bit difficult, because many were handwritten, or typewritten with hand-

written notes on the back or in the margins. It was hard and uncomfortable, but at that point we were all so fascinated that we didn't even care.

The funny thing is, the letters themselves weren't all that interesting. They were mostly . . . whiny, might be the best word for it. Page after page of complaints: Someone's car wouldn't start. The barn burned down. The bank was foreclosing on the house. The hired hand is a drunk and hasn't come to work for three days. My sister broke her ankle. Our daughter drowned. My cousin left town and won't pay back the debt he owes me.

Some told of tragedies, some recounted little more than the frustrations of a bad day. But all were pretty . . . ordinary. Just the ordinary bad news of life.

"What . . . what are these?" said Mom. "Why did people send this stuff to him? And how did it end up here?"

"It's Pronoica," said Raph in a low voice. "It's what we were looking for all along."

The question I had asked Raph in the library came back to me: If all the letters Williamson received were so positive, why did the house seem so dark and troubled? Now I understood—those weren't all the letters he received—those were just the ones he wanted people to know about.

"Williamson was a man with much to hide," said Verano. "It must have been daunting for him, trying to maintain this religion based around the premise that you can direct the universe to only hand you good things. I suspect that his technique worked for a while . . . but it was like a pendulum. There is only so far you can push it to one side, before it swings back in the other direction."

In the dim light cast by the flashlights, I saw Mom's eyes widen in horror. I knew what she was thinking. She was so like

276

Williamson—always believing the best of everyone, and that the universe itself had nothing but good intentions toward her. She believed as fervently as Williamson had that if she focused her energy on good things, good things would come to her. The idea that doing this was only delaying the time when an evil undertow would drag her back down with even greater intensity . . . the horror of the idea was inescapable.

"I have suspected for some time that Williamson was hiding something like this. Evidence that Pronoica was not the cure for all ills. The complaints in these letters may seem small, but the stakes were incredibly high for Williamson. His entire empire would have come crumbling down around him if people found out about this. So he hid them away. Desperation to find a secure place to store these letters must have been what led him to discover this space between the floors."

"And when Amelia became another liability," I said. "Another piece of bad news, he shut her up in here too."

"Guys," said Logan. "Look at this."

I thought he had picked up one of the letters and started to read it, but as I looked more closely, I saw that it wasn't a letter. It was an old school notebook, like kids might have used in the 1940s. It was filled with writing in a large, looping script. Raph grabbed it out of Logan's hands.

"What is it?" I said.

"Her journal," said Logan.

"Christ," said Raph. "It's got everything. The whole story. The clinic . . ." His eyes scanned the pages rapidly. Then he looked up. "Something did happen here. Something happened to Amelia."

Stopping and starting as he flipped through the pages for information, Raph gradually told us the story. The first few pages were ordinary enough: Amelia's concerns about school and hopes for her future. Only occasional mentions of her father's project, which didn't seem to interest her much. At least until he opened the clinic.

She was excited about that. Apparently a sweet-tempered, tenderhearted girl, she believed absolutely in her father's power as a healer, and looked forward to seeing the sick and crippled healed by his hand. He assembled a small crowd, brought them to remote Idaho, and invited her to attend his ritual. But as he stood before them, chanting and muttering and invoking the God power, something happened to Amelia. The way she put it, she was possessed by some spirit that took control of her body and mind and threw her to the ground, where she shook violently and made terrible noises.

She lost consciousness, and when she woke up, she was in this room—locked away, friendless, hopeless, all but forgotten, to live out the rest of her short life in forced seclusion. The only human interaction she had from then on was when a silent servant brought her meals, and when her father mounted the stairs from time to time to stow more letters away in the chest of her room, which he did without speaking to or even looking at her.

At first, the bad letters arrived only occasionally, but soon after the failure of the Pronoica Clinic, they began to increase in number and frequency. Family members of those who had attended the clinic wrote to Williamson to ask him what had happened. Ask him to explain to them why their loved ones had returned to them silent and stricken. What did he do to them? Not only were they not cured, they were worse than ever.

What had Williamson done to ensure their silence? Threats?

Blackmail? Hypnosis? Or did he wield the dangerous energy of Pronoica against them now, to suit his own ends?

But those were only the first letters. They dried up after a while, but were replaced by something far more sinister. Dozens and dozens of letters, many of them duplicates, some of them garbled, and others . . . Williamson hid those letters even more carefully, and Amelia could only guess at what they contained.

Raph eventually put the notebook down on top of the other letters, and even in nothing more than the glow from a flashlight, I could see how pale he was.

Behind me I could feel Mom trembling. "I think I'm going to be sick," she said. I thought she was being metaphorical, but a moment later she started to sway, and then she fell backward, catching herself with a hand grasping at one of the pads on the wall. It came free from the wall as she fell, and there was the sound of a loud rip. I rushed to her side to make sure she was okay, while Raph shone his flashlight on us.

"What's that behind them?" said Logan. "There's something behind the pads."

"My God," said Verano. The pool of light thrown by his flashlight swung around the room, casting us from light into darkness as he moved swiftly toward the torn cushion.

"Letters," he muttered as he dug his hand into the pile. "More letters." He started to tug the neighboring pads free from the walls, and as he did, more ancient, yellowed envelopes spilled into his hands. Raph picked a handful up from the floor and, holding them under his trembling light, he picked one from the bunch, carefully folded back the flap, and slid the decrepit paper free.

"Are you sure this is a good idea?" said Mom.

"What's it say?" said Logan.

"I—I have no idea," said Raph. I took a step closer to him and peered over his shoulder. The page between his fingers certainly looked like it had writing on it, but it was so tiny and crabbed that it was impossible to decipher. Here and there I could make out what appeared to be a letter, but I couldn't be sure whether they added up to true writing or were just the scribblings of the deranged.

"Try another," I said.

"Raphael, be careful," said Verano. "This isn't child's play. These letters need to be catalogued, properly preserved."

Raph ignored him and slipped a trembling finger under the aged seal of another. This one was even odder. It came out as a giant sheet but of a very strange shape. As the light shone on it and we got a better look, I saw that the page was constructed out of dozens of little scraps of paper—bits of receipts, paper bags, note cards, matchbook covers—all glued painstakingly together. Some of the scraps had typed writing, others hand-writing, others cartoonish pictures and abstract doodles. Again, I couldn't tell if it added up to anything meaningful, though there were actual words at least.

Raph put it down and picked up another.

He flicked open the flap on the envelope and reached his long, thin fingers in to pull stationary out, but this time it stuck. He tugged on it, gingerly at first, careful not to cause any dam-age, but gradually with more force, as his eagerness to know what was inside overcame his fastidious instincts. At last the page came free and Raph withdrew it, but as it slipped out, a soft black mass fell out into Raph's hand, followed by a col-lection of something small and dark that hit the floor with a delicate sound.

"What is it?" I said. Raph held his hand to his face to look more closely, then grunted and dropped the object, letting the flashlight clatter to the floor as well so its spotlight rolled along the far wall.

"Hair," he said, holding his sleeve to his mouth.

I grabbed the flashlight and focused it at the floor. In the middle of my beam lay a tangled black clump of human hair, like the refuse pulled from a hairbrush, while all around it were scattered an assortment of dark, crusted, concave disks. Logan put his fingers out and pressed them to the disks as if he was picking up crumbs from the kitchen table. He lifted his hand and turned it so we could all see.

"Is that . . . ?" said Mom. I knew, but my mouth had gone dry and my tongue felt too thick and heavy to speak. Logan said it for me.

"Fingernails," he said. "Bloody fingernails."

No one wanted to spend any more time up in that room. But we couldn't just walk away from it either. Somehow without really discussing it, we came to the unanimous conclusion that we needed to get the letters out of there. For ten minutes or so, as fast as we could, we worked together in silence, tearing down the pads and tossing handfuls and armfuls of the aging letters into the trunk that held the other, more normal ones. When we seemed to have gotten them all, Raph squeezed the lid on the trunk shut, and he and Mom each took a side and hauled it back out through the broken door and the hole in the wall, down the stairs, and placed it on the coffee table in the living room.

It was strange, though. The letters felt different sitting on the coffee table in the bright sunlight of a Tuesday morning in late spring. Very different from how they'd felt in that cold, dark room. Upstairs I was so shaken I wanted nothing to do with the letters, but now that they sat here like some kind of set dressing for a Restoration Hardware catalog shoot, all I wanted was to pore over them and examine every strange thing they contained.

I reached for one and started to fold up the flap.

"No way," came Mom's voice from the kitchen. "You put that down, Paige."

"Why?"

"Why? How are you even asking that? You saw what I saw. There's something . . . unhealthy in those letters, and reading them cannot be a good idea. What we need to do is get rid of them. Get them out of the house as soon as possible."

"We need to burn them," said Logan in a low, intense voice. He hadn't spoken since we came downstairs, and his voice came as a shock to me. I was still having some trouble reconciling this Logan with the one I saw last night, and figuring out which of the two—if either—was for real. The two versions blurred together before my eyes. "Mom's right. There's . . . nothing okay about these. We can't read them."

Mom clapped her hands together as if efficiently solving a problem. "Sounds fine to me. Let's just take them outside and burn them right now, and we can be done with it."

"No," said Verano. "I'm afraid I can't let you do that."

"It's my house," said Mom. "We found them here, so it's my property. I can do what I want with them, and I want them destroyed."

Verano struck the floor firmly with his cane. "It's my collection," he said with severe authority. "I am the curator of the Pronoica collection for the University of Idaho. All the pieces of that collection are my responsibility, including these. If the content of these letters does not interest you, that's your decision, but they must be exposed to the light of day. They have been hidden far too long. Repression of the unpleasant aspects of life is the root of the problem we face today. Williamson tried to silence these voices, but they were destined to return."

"With all due respect," said Mom, clearly fighting to keep her calm, "I'm not exactly convinced of your expertise in this field. I've been a student and practitioner of the magical arts for more than half my life, and I'm descended from a long line of acknowledged mystics. You—you're an academic kook trying to burnish your ego and your CV with this 'discovery,' and not thinking twice about the real lives you would ruin in the process. I know your kind, I deal with them every day. Big-name professors who say they want to help the environment, preserve the ecosystem, save the species, but all they really care about is winning the next grant so they can fund their sabbatical somewhere sunny. You come into my house with your academic credentials, but it's possible I know more than you about the shadow realm. Prying into these letters—it's unwholesome. They weren't meant to be read. We weren't meant to read them."

Professor Verano shook his head, a humorless smile on his face. "Ms. Blanton, it is very likely you who awakened this evil with your supposed mystical expertise. People have resided in this building for decades with no more than a slight degree of paranormal activity. Do you think it coincidence that you arrive in this town with your thaumaturlogical toys, some of them clearly far more powerful than you understand, and this house immediately begins its rebellion? The secrets, the grievances in these letters, must be exposed to the light, or they will fester and corrupt this place for generations to come."

For a moment, the two stood silent and bristling at each other, apparently at an impasse. Then Raph spoke. "You're both wrong," he said. "I'm sorry, Ms. Blanton, but you don't own this house. You rent. The house belongs to me."

"To your mom," I mumbled under my breath.

"Actually," he replied, "it's my name on the deed. For tax reasons my mom didn't want it in her name, and her lawyer suggested putting it in mine. So . . . legally speaking . . . the house is mine."

"Raphael," said Verano, a tinge of triumph in his voice already. "You understand, don't you? After all we've seen, all we've learned. You know how important these documents are. My work—*our* work. You won't let it all go to waste. We are exactly who is meant to read them. They are in our hands, aren't they? What better evidence could we ask for? A letter always arrives at its destination."

Raph hesitated a moment, then nodded. "Verano is right. The letters need to be preserved. And catalogued. Simply sitting down and reading them like some old love letters won't get us anywhere. What we need is data. We need a system. Some way to manage all the information and bring it into view."

"Yes," said Verano, growing excited. "Exactly, precisely right. Ah, Raphael, you are thinking like a historian now. We need to get the new documents to the library right away, where they can be—"

"No," said Raph. "Not yet. Like I said, they need to be sorted and catalogued. Monty—*Professor*. Who are you going to get to do that, some marketing major looking for a summer internship? What the hell are they going to know, or care, about this work? I've lived with Pronoica for more than a year now. I've scanned and catalogued every last piece of that collection for you, and checked it over twice. You said it yourself: No one knows this collection better than I do. Not even you."

"That's correct," said Verano. "But still, they belong at the library."

"Where I'll have no access to them. Thanks to you."

Professor Verano held Raph's stare for a long moment before looking away. "Yes, fine," he said, as if Raph had just brought up a particularly distasteful subject. "You have a point. All right then, we'll work on them here."

"No," said Raph again. "That is . . . I'd rather you didn't. It seems like a bad idea." Verano didn't answer, but his brow was furrowed, his expression dark. At last he nodded. Apparently deciding that this compromise solution was better than the likely alternative, he limited himself to giving some very precise instructions to Raph with regards to the database and its finer points, then grabbed his cane and swept out the door.

As soon as Verano left, Mom jumped on Raph, repeating again how she didn't want the letters in her house for one minute longer, etc. etc. I guess she thought Raph would be easier to break down than Verano, and . . . well, she was right, kind of. Because he brushed her off immediately, saying, "Don't worry, Ms. Blanton. I have no intention of keeping these letters around. Logan was right—we're going to burn them."

He explained that there was no way Verano would ever leave the letters with them unless he thought they were perfectly safe, so he had to let him believe that he would preserve them. But then he called Verano a "damned obsessive" who couldn't see past his own ego. And it's true that Verano knows the least of all of us what we've been living through these past months, so how could he possibly understand?

Anyway, Logan was all set to dump the stuff in a pile outside and light a match to it right then and there—if not just start a fire right on the coffee table—but Arthur arrived just in time with a more sensible suggestion. Good old Arthur . . . He was driving up from Lapwai with dinner from CD's barbecue restaurant for everyone, and walked in on what must have looked like a very strange scene. But he took it all in with his usual aplomb.

"Hey, now," he said, "you can't start a fire here. There's a burn ban on."

"A what?" I said.

"A burn ban," said Arthur. "Have you seen the conditions out there? It's hot and dry and windy, and the slightest spark could set off a massive wildfire. Starting any kind of fire now would be—"

Raph rolled his eyes. "Yes, I know all about the burn ban. Look, I've lived here all my life. I've been through a zillion fire seasons. It just means you have to be careful. And I know how to take precautions."

Arthur and Mom were silent. Worried.

"I'm not talking about hosting a barbecue, or starting a bonfire just for fun. This is important. What do you want to do, throw all this creepy shit in the Dumpster outside? Bring it down to the recycling center? Do you really think that's going to solve the problem? We need to purge this stuff. Purge the house. Fire is the only way we're going to do that."

Mom looked to Arthur, who hesitated before giving a nod. "We do it on the rez sometimes—get special dispensations for ritual fires. There are some things only a fire can cleanse. But Jesus, you have to be very, very careful. Will you at least wait until tonight, and let me do it with you?"

Raph agreed to this, so I guess we get to put off our big creepy bonfire a few more hours.

WEDNESDAY, JUNE 17, 12:43 A.M.

Raph was right. I am so glad we did burn them.

God, I . . . I feel better than I have since . . . well, since before we first moved into this house. It's crazy how different everything feels just as a result of that one act. Suddenly I can walk around this house without feeling like I'm carrying a heavy load all the time. I didn't even realize until now how much it was affecting me, but right now I just feel so light and free and . . . peaceful. At last. This house, which has brought us all so much trouble and pain, it is just a house now. It's old, and it still has a lot of history, but . . . that's all it is now. History. It's not living with us and feeding on us and fucking with us anymore.

But I should back up and describe what happened. We waited until dark, which felt like forever. But finally the sun set, and Arthur and Raph went about digging a deep hole in the gravel driveway outside. I'd invited Chloe to sleep over, since I knew she would want to see this story through to the end. Once she got here, she, Logan, and I wandered around the fields just past the property, looking for large stones and bringing them back to the hole by the armful. We made a ring of big stones around the pit, and cleared the area of any dry, inflammable objects—twigs and leaves and stuff. Then at last we lugged the big, overstuffed trunk outside, and started tossing the unread letters into the pit by the handful. They didn't all fit easily, so we decided to do it in batches. Arthur lit another branch of patosway and held it in the air a few moments, humming the same song his grandfather had sung the other time. He seemed a lot less comfortable with it, though, as if it were something he only half remembered. Then he dropped the patosway into the pit, and almost instantly the old, dried-out envelopes began to blacken and smoke. Before long, small flames erupted and the pages started to curl, and then the fire started in earnest, curling the letters into ash. The wind was picking up, but we were very careful to control the ash and keep it from drifting up into the air on a gust. We had covers we could put on it if it seemed to be getting too big, and we kept it very controlled.

Even so, this carefully tended fire had a feeling of purging about it. The pungent smell of the patosway drifted through the air, and the black smoke curled into the sky to meet with the terrible cloud of fire debris already hanging over the city, almost as if it was returning home. Periodically we threw more letters onto the fire and allowed them to burn themselves out into ash. While we waited, Mom went inside and got blankets and lawn chairs so we could be a bit more comfortable. Lying on a blanket with Raph, staring up at the orange moon, it was almost possible

to forget what we were actually doing. It was more like we were all on a summer camping trip than trying to rid our house of demonic possession.

Toward midnight, the final batch of letters was at last settling down into a heap of slightly smoking ash, and Arthur began covering it with dirt and gravel, to smother the remains of the fire and make sure it couldn't spread.

At that point Mom caught my eye and nodded toward Logan, and . . . it was the most amazing thing. He was sleeping! Deeply and peacefully. I think that, more than anything, convinced me that this time our ritual really worked and that we could all go back to normal. It made me so happy that tears sprang to my eyes. But Mom just smiled and put her fingers to her lips. She got up and scooped him into her arms like she used to when he was a little kid. He did really look like a little kid again, his face innocent in the dim light shining from the house windows.

Mom went inside to carry him up to bed. Arthur lingered a bit longer to make sure there wasn't the slightest trace of smoke, and then he followed her in with only a wink and a word to us not to stay up too late.

Chloe was the next to go. She had been sitting almost on the opposite side of the fire, and I could hardly pick her out of the shadows except for the glittering of her eyes in the firelight. She hadn't spoken in a while, but as Arthur disappeared into the house, she stood up and looked at us, saying she was going to turn in too. But she didn't leave right away—she just stood there, looking at us, her brow furrowed in that puzzle-solving expression of hers.

"Are you going to be okay?" she said at last.

"We're fine," I said, but she didn't move. She was looking really intensely at Raph.

"I'll be okay," he said. At this, she finally left us alone.

Honestly, I was so sleepy and exhausted by this point that I almost joined them and went up to bed. But another part of me didn't want this beautiful moment to end—the stars, the light wind, the warm night, the sense that I was finally safe and free from all that negative energy. And Raph lying beside me, sharing it with me . . .

Raph.

I sensed a nervous movement at my side, and suddenly Chloe's comment made more sense to me. In a blink the past 24 hours came flooding back to me. The spiders, my freak-out, Raph offering me his couch, me getting into his bed while he was sleeping . . . and then the horror that came after, the blood and fear and I still didn't know exactly what had happened. Had he told her?

I felt Raph shift again beside me, and wondered if he was trying to leave. Trying to escape politely. If he was scared to be around me.

I turned my head toward him, but he was still lying on his back, staring up at the sky. "Raph," I said. He didn't look at me, just kept staring straight up, but I could feel his muscles tense up a bit on the other side of the blanket. At last he sat up.

"I should get to bed," he said, and almost like an afterthought, he yawned extravagantly. I nodded, feeling like it wasn't my place to pressure him to stay. Especially if I was the one making him uncomfortable. But the very idea of that was making me feel pretty terrible.

He got up, brushed off his jeans, and started to move toward his basement door. I called out his name again and he stopped and turned.

"I'm sorry," I said. Raph sighed and ruffled his curls. In the dim starlight I couldn't make out even a trace of the injury that had been done to his lip last night, but I knew it was there, and the thought of it burned in my heart.

"I know," he said.

"Can you tell me what happened? I don't even—"

But Raph shook his head. "Don't think about it. You're better off not knowing. That wasn't you last night. This house . . . it's made us all a little crazy."

He gave me a little smile, and I smiled back. Then he went back to his apartment, and I folded the blanket and came up here to type this. But this story is over and my bed is calling to me.

I almost can't believe I won't have this weird shit to write about anymore. Believe me, I am not going to miss it! Maybe I will stop using this journal from now on. Or at least take a long break.

All I know is, if I ever log into the journal again, I hope my big excitement is who asked me to prom or where I got into college or something. That sounds . . . really nice right now.

WEDNESDAY, JUNE 17, 3:09 A.M.

It's 3 a.m. and I'm awake. Again. What woke me up? I don't know. Chloe is still sleeping peacefully in the other bed, but my skin is prickling and I feel wide-awake. Alert. I thought . . . I don't know, I thought I heard . . . or felt . . . shaking? But I don't feel it now. I do smell something, though. Burning. It doesn't smell close, but I can feel it in my lungs again.

Hmm, I just checked the local news, and I guess there is a wildfire just outside of town. I hope this has nothing to do with our fire earlier. God, wouldn't that be awful. But the website seemed to think it was caused by a lightning strike, and it is pretty far away. Anyway, it sounds like the firefighters have it pretty much under control.

I still feel nervous and unquiet, though. I think I will go quickly check on Logan, just to calm my nerves.

WEDNESDAY, JUNE 17, 6:32 A.M.

Shit. Shit. I don't know what's going on. Is it all starting again? Will we never be free of this . . . whatever it is?

I found Logan lying in a patch of sunlight, shaking and drooling and choking—another seizure. And my heart just . . . fell. Because as awful as it is to see your baby brother suffering like that, what made it even worse was the sinking feeling that our ritual didn't work, that whatever evil was in this house is still here, is still messing with us. And it's getting worse.

But I just don't know. Maybe the seizure is unrelated? How can we be sure?

I called out for Mom, but I didn't want to leave Logan alone, so I ran over to him. I called again, but no one seemed to be coming, so I just . . . calmed myself down and tried to remember the stuff they taught us about how to deal with a seizure.

I rolled him onto his side and put a pillow under his head, and that seemed to help. He stopped shaking, anyway. So then I just sat there and rubbed his back and soothed him, and eventually he fell back to sleep.

That's when Arthur came in, finally. He saw me there and looked really freaked out as I tried to explain to him calmly and quietly (so as not to wake up Logan) what had happened. But for some reason he just stared at me and Logan, looking horrified. Even though we were clearly out of the woods. But he must have realized the same thing I did: if Logan is convulsing again, it must mean that the house is still haunted.

Eventually he got himself together and went to get my mom. I stayed with Logan until Mom came. She looked really freaked out too, and ran right to his side, crying and sobbing. I tried to calm her down, but she wasn't paying attention to me. I guess I can understand why she panicked, after all we've been through.

By then, Arthur was on the phone, and I figured I was probably doing more harm than good by hanging out there, so I went back to my room to write this up. Ugh, so much for getting to put this journal to rest! Now I don't know what will happen.

I'm so exhausted, but I don't want to go back to sleep when things are like this. Wait, how did it get to be morning already? The past couple of days have really scrambled my brain. I'm going to go downstairs to make some coffee.

WEDNESDAY, JUNE 17, 12:50 P.M.

~~Every atomic spirit is through the statement of us, is discovery~~
~~than problem come~~

I'm in the room. Amelia's room.

~~in the atomic above. The spirit the statement spirit, in invis-~~
~~ible fast more power~~

The cell. It's not padded anymore, since we tore down all
the cushions on the walls. But it is small and dark and locked.

~~of race, than through at the before through billion the one~~
~~body the~~

Writing on my phone, which keeps glitching up, so who
knows if this will work. But I have to do something, have to
record this somehow.

~~energy spirit, by becoming one one of the answer than the~~
~~billion invisible the existence spirit,~~

Maybe it's stupid to use my phone to make a journal entry right now. Maybe I should use it to call the police and get me the hell out of here. But what good would that do? So I could trade one cell for another? A jail cell. Or if everyone decides I'm as nuts as I seem to be, maybe I could upgrade to a cell that still has its padding. And a nice straitjacket to go with it.

the ever existence in closer.

Hardly sounds like an improvement.

The invisible are waiting for you, you

I need to back up and explain how I got here.

follow WANT spirit is that everything waiting intelligence. Please

I went downstairs to make coffee, still emotionally overwhelmed and mentally fried from exhaustion and worry about Logan. I picked up the pot and ran it under the tap for a second before I noticed something weird. There was something in the coffeepot.

untold is you the intelligence. Follow your power, and follow in the studies,

A letter.

and invisible spirit IS FOR everything

Why would a letter be in the coffeepot? Well, why not? After everything else that's gone on in this house, why the fuck not?

recognize closely YOU

I turned off the water. My fingers trembling, I pulled the letter from the pot, opened it, and started to read. Tried to read. All the words were blacked out—every single one. You could tell how long each word was, more or less, but that's it. They were all scratched out to invisibility.

they ARE the intelligence.

Something else I noticed: bloody fingerprints in the margins, bright red and smeary.

YOU invisible invisible very spirit of YOU untold invisible

I don't know how long I stood there, staring down at the letter in my hands in blank confusion, before I was brought back to myself by a voice.

These waiting presence. Power. Invisible day,

"You tried to destroy them, didn't you?"

the ever you spirit in YOU FOR wealth, presence, everything.

I looked up. Professor Verano was standing in the doorway to the house, leaning hard against his cane, his face twisted in fury. I couldn't answer him at first, so he stepped inside and walked slowly forward to meet me in the kitchen, limping heavily.

in atomic World the than invisible of in spirit invisible in

He stopped a couple of steps away from me.

FOR spirit, in the can statement intelligence. fast invisible Please ARE than Invisible Living

"I told you not to," he said, his voice shaking with barely suppressed rage, "but you did it anyway. You tried to destroy the letters."

spirit you come closer

I looked down at the letter in my hand, then back up at his face. "We did destroy them," I said. "We had a bonfire. We threw them all in. Every one."

The these presence. presence, than waiting intelligence. that FOR intelligence

"Then explain this." Verano reached into his coat and pulled out a sheaf of letters, which he thrust toward me. Not just any letters—old, yellowed. Curled around the edges. Unmistakably the Pronoica letters.

~~problem Living Every for everything Please invisible in recognize Power. Spirit closer.~~

"You saved some," I said. "You stole them from the trunk and took them with you, and then you broke in here and planted this here to freak me out."

~~The spirit, in spirit by is presence. problem atomic intelligence.~~

Verano smiled grimly and shook his head. "I didn't save anything. I trusted you. I trusted Raph. Trusted him to follow my instructions and not do anything rash. Then these turned up under my pillow this morning. Another one was in the umbrella stand. Five more in the glove compartment of my car. They're probably all over town by now," he said. He looked at me sharply, intently, his cold eyes cutting right through me. "You should have listened to me," he said, his voice quiet but laced with menace. He took a step forward. "I did warn you. You can't eradicate something like this, you can only repress it. But the repressed object will always, inevitably return."

~~one invisible waiting for untold one body before The by waiting Every the invisible in~~

I backed away from him until I hit the counter. There was something unsettling about the way he was looking at me, but I couldn't figure out what it meant. Something was distracting me. A noise, like screaming. Shrieking. That sound from Logan's room, the sound of someone wailing in agony.

~~can these everything waiting waiting YOU is come invisible invisible~~

"It doesn't make any sense," I said. "It was supposed to be all over. It was supposed to be better now."

very is invisible the follow ever Every follow are Power.

Verano turned toward the sound of footsteps clomping down the stairs, and a moment later, Arthur came into view, and he let out a cry as he reached the kitchen. I'd never seen him like this before. Good, kind, sensible Arthur was advancing toward me like a madman. Sweat was pouring from his face, and he was also holding a towel to his side, a large red splotch darkening and spreading through the terry cloth. A second later, my mom appeared, her face red and tear streaked. She threw herself at Arthur, tugging him back with clawlike fingers.

Power. statement FOR you, everything at power closer.

"Don't," she wailed. "Don't touch her."

at invisible the invisible ever and the than the these spirit the is of that

"Mom?" I said, struggling to pull the information gathered by my senses into any coherent order. "What's going on? How is Logan? Is he awake yet?"

the atomic be and the atomic atomic you discovery of that The discovery Spirit

Mom didn't answer, but her face crumpled into desperate sobs before my eyes, and she continued to wrestle wordlessly with Arthur. Only then did I realize that Chloe was in the kitchen too. Her face was paler than usual, but otherwise she seemed almost eerily impassive next to Mom and Arthur.

that The everything invisible blood problem the everything. is come

"Logan's dead," she said flatly.

body invisible recognize invisible FOR atomic in one spirit abundance

I was speechless for a moment. Mom and Arthur also froze at her words, looking at me with strange fear on their faces. I looked to them desperately, waiting for them to say something, to contradict her, to call her way out of line for joking about something like that. But they didn't.

~~on follow in you invisible everything the is Spirit Every atomic problem~~

"No," I said. "No, I saved his life, I sat with him, I did all the things you're supposed to." But still they didn't answer. Into the silence that had descended on the kitchen, Arthur let out another roar and lunged for me again. He winced in pain as Mom held him back by his shoulder.

"What happened?" I said, my voice coming out broken and raw. "What happened?" I repeated more loudly when no one answered.

~~Power. Invisible becoming the than~~

That's when things started to come together. Pieces of the puzzle attaching themselves to one another in my mind. "It has something to do with the house, doesn't it? Amelia. The letters. The evil that's locked in this place. Something got to him." I looked around and for the first time, noticed something missing. "Where is Raph?" I clapped a hand to my mouth as realization overtook me. "No," I said. "No, it can't . . . Dr. Clyde was right. She warned me. She told me Raph was dangerous. Told me I should stay away from him. But it was too late. His experiments . . . all that good luck he thought he was buying, but it was only borrowed. He tried to cover his mistake by burning those letters, but instead he awakened something. Unleashed some power, some uncontrollable force—"

~~statement invisible in of ever may tail atomic perfect~~

Finally Chloe's calm, hard voice broke through my babbling.

~~Invisible and is through studies, of follow the of The the abundance.~~

"You really don't remember?"

~~spirit, is everything. discovery on spirit power, presence, blood spirit at the perfect spirit~~

I swallowed. "Remember what?"

~~Please the you World the than ever Please everything~~

Chloe took the last few steps into the kitchen and approached me, stepping around Arthur. "It's not Raph," she said slowly. "It's you. It's been you all along. You're the one who disturbed the spirits . . . They had always been here, resting fitfully, waiting for someone to come along and awaken them. Someone whose cryptic power had been concentrated through many generations. Someone with a force that resonated with theirs. A conductor of dark energy.

~~YOU waiting IS the answer~~

"You never guessed? I knew . . . almost since I met you. I couldn't believe that you didn't know yourself. And your mom . . ." Chloe turned toward her. "You must have seen the signs. But then, a mother's love. You wouldn't let yourself acknowledge it."

~~Every existence of race, and may the very everything race, very~~

"What the hell is she talking about?" I said. Mom let out another wail.

~~the the of tail of spirit the untold invisible~~

Verano turned to Arthur. "I think it's time we call the police."

~~the in before atomic you in at The energy the closely Power.~~

"No," said Mom fiercely. She turned on Verano with a vicious expression on her face. "I won't let you. You know what will happen if you do. They'll take her. I've lost one baby already today. I won't let them take the other."

Spirit waiting you the are is the the spirit, race, you the World

"We can't just let her alone," gritted Arthur through clenched teeth. It was eerie to have them discuss me like that, right in front of me. I could almost believe they were talking about someone else. "She's dangerous. She's a danger to herself, and to all of us."

presence, the invisible the you waiting one existence spirit, FOR everything abundance

"*I* am?" I said. "No, you don't understand. It was Raph. He was the one who brought all this into the house. The one who awoke the spirits."

spirit, atomic these in in power problem

"Raph may have had some part in it," said Verano, "but he didn't deserve . . ." Verano's face darkened with violent emotion, and he couldn't go on.

WANT

"I don't understand," I said. "Where is he? Where is Raph?"

presence. invisible energy FOR body

"Dead," said Verano.

Every you the the recognize follow more intelligence. us, energy Invisible the FOR tail

This was a dream. This had to be a horrible dream. "Raph and Logan? How can that be?"

The IS of statement untold the IS of invisible is you bring in ever untold of of the

"Paige," said Chloe, "look at yourself."

we will know you beyond the tomb

So I did. I still clenched that mysterious letter . . . . My hands, my arms, my clothes were all drenched in blood.

ignoring spiritual absence takes failure sickness misery,

"I can't lose them both," Mom was repeating to herself, almost like a chant, while I tried to make sense of the information I was absorbing. "She wasn't in her right mind when she killed them," she said. "It's not her fault. I have to protect her."

the absent flesh of the devil is the finite result of all our gifts,

"Arthur is right. If we leave her be, she'll kill again," said Verano.

stone embodied lies, the dead will bring you

"Then lock her in the room," said Chloe. "Amelia's room. She'll be safe there. We'll all be safe."

what you want don't want abundance abundance abundance abundance, ignoring spiritual absence takes

And so here I am. I went quietly, after all that. What was the point in resisting? I could see the truth in what they said. If it's true—that I snuck down into Raph's apartment last night and stabbed him in his sleep, then came back upstairs and strangled Logan—how can I argue with their decision? I'm a menace. Dr. Clyde was right all along. I just couldn't let myself see what she was trying to tell me. She kept telling me that the house was a distraction. That my worry for Logan was a kind of deflection. That I should focus on myself. I thought she was telling me to stay away from Raph because he was dangerous, but no. It was *me*. Raph kept telling me there was a danger in us hanging out together. I was so blind. So sure that he meant he was a danger to me, which I didn't believe, because I couldn't imagine him ever being a danger to anyone. And he wasn't. I was.

failure sickness misery, the absent flesh of the devil is the finite result of all our gifts.

And my mom's stories of the mysticism of our ancestors . . . I pushed them away for so many years because they contained a truth I wasn't ready to accept. This year, when I finally started to listen, I still only heard what I wanted to. That we were on the side of good, that everyone who saw darkness in us was prejudiced and ignorant. But Chloe saw it. This house was restless before we came, but I'm the one who woke it up. Who acted as a conduit for all the bad history sitting here. As long as I'm here, I'm only making it worse.

the devil everyone forgets.

But what do I do? What do I do now? How can I end it all? There has to be a way.

WEDNESDAY, JUNE 17, 10:43 P.M.

There is a way. I understand now. The house showed it to me. I was standing here, alone in the middle of this room, shaking and sobbing with guilt and fear, and then . . . I can't explain it. But that's nothing new. There is so much I can't explain about my life these past six months. I just have to accept it.

I saw the land spread out around me. The town and the fields and the barns and the big empty sky. I saw it all, even though I was shut up in that tiny dark room. It was like the walls on every side of me just fell away, and I could turn in a circle and see every little feature of the landscape spread out around me.

And it was on fire. The smoke started to roll in off the fields, choking my breath and making my eyes water. I could feel the particles of ash and debris in the air, feel the wind moving the flames inexorably forward.

That's when I understood. Burning is purging. Purifying. The witch hunters who feared my ancestors knew the cleansing properties of fire, and they weren't wrong. This fire around me is a gift. I must go to it—I must leave this prison and seek it out. It's the only way I can end this. The only way I can repair the evil I have wrought.

Wildfire Ravages Moscow Neighborhood

An uncontrolled wildfire spread to the outskirts of Moscow and laid waste to a neighborhood to the northwest of town. A number of houses and apartment complexes were engulfed in flames, and firefighters are still working to control the blaze. Fire Chief Mathers expressed his belief that the conflagration would soon be under control, and they could begin assessing damage.

At the moment, only one fatality of an unknown female has been established, who was seen by witnesses to jump from the window of a house and run toward the approaching fire. Police are currently investigating this story.

A few structures are still burning, and around a dozen people are homeless tonight. One house, however, which was in the direct path of the fire, emerged unscathed. Many are calling it a miracle that this Moscow landmark and one of the oldest houses in the city survived perfectly intact even as many of the neighboring houses succumbed to the out-of-control wildfire.

AFTERWORD

I find I have little to add to the story as it appears in these pages, and yet some details bear clarifying as much as is possible. In truth, there is little certainty to be gleaned in the aftermath of this terrible event.

As to the source of the unrest in the old house, I believe I have made my own position adequately clear. My conclusions, however, are not shared by all, and I would be remiss if I did not mention the most compelling alternative explanation.

Dr. Louisa Clyde has testified in court that Paige Blanton was suffering from a constellation of psychological disorders that, in the early morning hours of the 17th, caused her to take the lives of two people and make an attempt on a third. Paige's repressed rage toward her father in the aftermath of his infidelity manifested as aggression toward her little brother. Raphael came to represent in her mind her own failure to live up to the model of adult feminine sexuality provided by her mother, while Mr. Taylor she resented as a rival for her mother's affections.

As satisfying as this version of events has proven for the local police force, it still leaves some unanswered questions. For example, it has been demonstrated conclusively that Paige's phone, with which she supposedly made these last journal entries, was not on her person when she died, nor was it left in the room where Paige had been temporarily secured. Rather, it had been abandoned on the kitchen table when Paige was forcibly restrained, and it remained there hours later.

There are those who fixate on this strange detail as proof of some great conspiracy in this matter. A more common theory is that Chloe is the de facto author of the last few entries in the journal, while smaller factions point fingers in other directions, blaming Ms. Blanton, Mr. Taylor, or even myself as perpetrators of a supposed hoax.

For my own part, I don't pretend to have any explanation that fits into a rational narrative of the events. I leave it to the reader to draw his or her own conclusions.

TURN THE PAGE FOR A SNEAK PEEK AT

ANOTHER HAUNTING DIARY . . .

All her life, Laetitia has wanted to be a star. It's more than an ambition—somewhere deep inside, she feels certain that she was born for greatness.

But the path to stardom now seems to be halted by the mysterious undiagnosed illness that's taken over her body. Doctors don't have a clue what could be causing it. She stays home from school most days, documenting her strange symptoms. Symptoms that start with fevers and chills, but soon escalate to strange items her body seems to be producing—bones, nails, and even glass.

All the while, Laetitia is fixated on what is happening in the news: race riots that are moving ever closer to her neighborhood. But when visions of horrific scenes begin to invade her mind, even the media can't distract her.

As Laetitia's illness worsens, she soon begins to wonder—is her sickness biological, or is it something more? Are the voices she hears signs of insanity—or signs of something much more sinister and demonic? Or, perhaps, signs of something more benevolent . . . something holy?

Laetitia always knew she'd be a star . . . she just never knew how quickly it would all manifest.

Thank you all for your comments on my last tutorial on creating a two-tone wig! I'm glad it was useful. And you know, you can use that same technique to create more than two tones if you want to do three tones or go crazy and do, like, a million different colors. Actually, that would be difficult—you probably want to limit yourself to four or five at most.

And thanks to everyone who said I looked fabulous! You guys are the best.

(*→‿←*) <-- *blushing*

Sometimes people at school or on the street try to judge me for having pink or purple or turquoise hair, or wearing glittery eyelashes in the middle of the afternoon, but screw them.

You guys understand me and always know how to lift my spirits.

Speaking of which, today was rough. I lost my voice! Totally and completely lost it—I opened my mouth, and nothing at all came out. I panicked, of course. That's never happened to me before. . . . . I've had sore or scratchy throats, and I've gotten hoarse, but never anything like this. Completely out of the blue. I can talk a little if I force it—croak like a frog, really. But what good does croaking do me when I'm supposed to be rehearsing every day? The open auditions for *America Sings* are only a few months away, and I definitely can't sing like this.

It's really stressing me out. I *have* to make that audition! When am I ever going to get another chance like this? A chance to sing in front of real TV producers from Hollywood? I need this. I know if they can just hear me, they will love me. But I *need* to be at that audition.

I've been working at this for so long. My whole life, really. And I can practice and post videos online and do all the little church solos I want, but none of that is going to make me a star. It's not enough to sing just for the people here, in my neighborhood, or the handful of people reading my blog. I want the whole world to hear my voice. And for the longest time, I didn't see how I was going to make that happen. No matter how bad you want something, you can't just will it into existence.

But with these auditions coming up, I feel like I finally have a chance. I'm not worried about my voice or my talent. . . . Mostly I'm worried about getting up there and freezing, and blowing my only shot at being famous. That's why I've been rehearsing so much.

I got permission to use the school auditorium when no one else is, and I go in there and stand in front of all those empty seats and force myself to imagine those bigwigs from Hollywood judging me and making me feel small and insignificant. And I focus all my energy on showing them I am *not* small or insignificant—in letting them see the real ~**laetitia**~. The one who has a date with destiny.

But I can't do it without my voice! That's kind of an important part of being a singer.

I've never experienced anything like this before, even in a nightmare. Gramma Patty says it's just a cold, nothing to worry about, and I want to believe her, but I've got to admit I'm a little nervous. My head keeps filling with all these horrible things it could be—polyps, cancer—but Gramma Patty made me gargle with salt water when I got home (blech), and now I have some hot tea with honey, and it does seem to be helping a bit. I'm going to get some rest, and hopefully, it will all be better in the morning.

In the meantime, I would really appreciate any thoughts and prayers you can send my way. This is *so* important to me, and I can use all the support I can get. Thank you!!! I love you all so much.

(/◕ヮ◕)/*:・ﾟ✧

TUESDAY, JANUARY 7, 4:12 P.M. (PUBLIC)

Thank you for all the get-well-soon notes! I checked my messages this morning, and I was overwhelmed! You guys are the greatest.

I'm happy to say my voice is much better. There were one or two creaky moments when I was rehearsing after school, but nothing like yesterday. Hallelujah.

° · ✿ ˇ\(｡ ๑‿ ๑｡)/✿ ·˚

I was so happy I could talk and sing again, I decided to do an extraspecial ~*divanation*~ to celebrate. A pink-and-lavender wig with sparkly barrettes! Hope you like.

[photo redacted]

[photo redacted]

Since I got some new followers recently, I should explain: *divanation* is a word my best friend, Angela, made up when we were eleven, I think. It means "the process of making myself up like a diva." Turning plain old Laetitia into ~**laetitia**~, the fabulous diva who's going to rule the world with the power of her voice. I know it's silly, but it helps me be bold and confident to have this persona I put on every day. And it makes people treat me differently too. Back when I would go to school, looking ordinary, that's how everyone treated me. When I told them I was going to be a famous singer someday, they'd laugh or give me pitying looks. But when I put in a little effort every morning to look ~fabulous~, suddenly my dreams don't seem so crazy anymore. Now all my friends and teachers and everyone look at me like they see the person I am on the inside. Like they believe I'm capable of anything. And that helps, especially on days when I'm not so sure of it myself.

MONDAY, JANUARY 13, 4:17 P.M. (PUBLIC)

It happened again! My voice disappeared. Now I am seriously worried. (✿ ◉_◉)

Last time, I woke up the next morning and felt 1,000 percent better, and I was *so* relieved. I could talk again! And more important, I could sing! Praise be, etc. I didn't know if it was a cold or what, but all I cared about was that it was over. A little part of me wondered if that day of loss was meant to remind me to appreciate my gifts and not take them for granted, and I didn't! I went back to my rehearsing with new gratitude, and for five days everything was just fine.

Then today I got up there on the stage, opened my mouth, and *nothing*. I came straight home, and Gramma Patty sent me to bed again. She says I pushed myself too hard and didn't give myself a chance to fully recover. Maybe it's true—I do feel kind of awful. Last time it was just my voice, like someone had flicked a switch and turned it off but left the rest of me just fine. This time it's definitely more than that. I feel . . . run-down. Exhausted. A little achy, maybe. I wonder if I have a slight fever. I had strange dreams last night, and this morning I felt so low, I actually thought about going to school without doing my ~divanation~. But I can't do that—you have to have standards. And it's what people expect from me. The whole school might become demoralized if I showed up in plain braids.

Gramma Patty just brought me some more tea, and now that I've written all this out, I'm feeling a little calmer. Maybe this is just a message that I've been pushing myself too hard, and I need to rest for a while. I'm going to sleep early tonight, and I'm going to take a whole week off from singing, even if my voice comes back. That should help, and one week isn't really going to set me back for the audition. I have to remember to take care of myself.

TUESDAY, JANUARY 14, 6:15 A.M. (PUBLIC)

I just had the most terrible nightmare. I don't even know how to describe it. I know, I know, no one ever wants to hear someone describe their dreams, but . . . this wasn't like a normal dream. Not even like a normal nightmare. It was so clear and vivid—not all mixed up and confusing, the way my dreams usually are.

There wasn't really any story to it. All I remember was I was strapped down so I couldn't move at all. At first I thought I was on some kind of bed, but it wasn't really a bed. . . . It was more of an iron grate. I wasn't scared or anything. I was just like, *Oh, I guess this is what's happening now.* But then I realized someone was lighting a fire under the grate. Under *me*. And it started to get hotter and hotter until I could feel the flames tickling my skin.

And it *hurt*. I thought things weren't supposed to hurt

in dreams! I don't think I've ever experienced pain in a dream before, except when something also hurt me in real life (like when I fell out of bed that one time). But this wasn't like that. It was like I was being burned all over my body, and I could *feel* it—my skin blistering and crackling like a roasted pig.

But I didn't scream. I didn't do anything to try to save myself. Not that there was much I could have done, but I don't remember crying or struggling. It was just me and that grate and the fire. And the pain.

Then I opened my eyes and I was in my bed. I never even had a sense of waking up. It was just like I'd been living through this horrible thing, with my eyes closed, and when I opened them, I was back to myself.

I don't know. I know it was just a dream, but it shook me up, I guess. It was just so real. Part of me still feels like it really happened, even though I know that's impossible.

TUESDAY, JANUARY 14, 6:25 A.M. (PUBLIC)

That was weird.

I just got done writing up and posting my dream, but when I reloaded the page, there was this other post I don't remember making already on the blog. I mean, I *definitely* did not make that post. It was time-stamped from the middle of the night—when I was asleep!

It was just some weird photo. I have no clue where it came from. Some kind of glitch with the website, I guess? Wires crossed? ¯_(ツ)_/¯ I don't even know if that's possible, lol. But I don't know where else it could have come from, so I guess that must be it.

Anyway, I deleted it as soon as I saw it. I'm sorry if any of you out there saw it before I caught it! That's not the kind of thing I usually post at all.

I was going to just delete that photo from the other post, but I decided to save it first. Just in case it's not a glitch. Like if it's someone who has hacked my blog and is trying to mess with me, maybe. I don't know who would do that, but you never know. . . . All kinds of crazies out there.

I thought it might be smart to save it in a locked post in case I ever needed to show it as evidence or something.

I didn't notice before, because I was panicking about a strange pic on my blog and whether it would upset people and cost me followers, but now that I look at it again, it kind of reminds me of my dream, and that metal grill I was strapped to. Isn't that strange? I mean, it must just be a coincidence. What else could it be? Gives me the shivers either way, though.

Hey, everyone!

I just wanted to let everybody know I'm doing okay. Thank you all for your concern. I have gotten soooo many nice messages from people since my last couple of posts. You guys are the best, seriously. I know I've been kind of down lately and not like myself—some of you were worried about that dream I had, and then there was that weirdness with the picture—but you don't have to worry. I'm getting better, and I'll be back to your regularly scheduled ~divanation~ posts before you know it.

It's nice to know you care—I love you all!

Also, I hate to bring this up, but to the people who felt the need to send anon messages complaining about the "turn this blog has taken" and threatening to unfollow . . . yeah, I didn't appreciate that. This blog is a labor of love, and I haven't been feeling well, so that means I haven't been able to post my usual stuff. If hearing real stuff about what's going on in my life bothers you so much, go ahead and unfollow. Fine by me.

Okay, sorry about that. It was only a few people, but it had to be said.

Thanks again for your notes and messages! I love you all.